THE CASIQUE FAMILY

Us Before Anything 2

BRII TAYLOR

An Urban Love Story

CONTENTS

Facebook: *Brii Taylor*
Facebook Like Page: *Ms. Brii*
Instagram: *authoressbriitaylor*
Twitter: *taylor_brii*
Email: *authoressbrii@yahoo.com*
Website: www.justbriitaylor.com
Join my reader's group to keep up with new/upcoming releases,
get sneak peeks, giveaways and more!

CHAPTER 1

RELL

A few hours later…

Coming to, I had a banging headache. I couldn't remember shit that happened. Rubbing my head, I glanced at the clock on the dashboard. It was past 2 o'clock in the afternoon.

One thing I did remember was Keyona had a doctor's appointment. I'd scheduled it the other night. We were going to see how far along she was. She made a big fuss, but that didn't mean a damn thing to me. I needed to see what was up with the little me growing on the inside of her.

"What the…fuck?" I continued to rub the back of my head and look around in a daze. Keyona wasn't in the car, but her door was wide open. Mine was too.

Where the fuck is Keyona? That's what I wanted to know. Slowly, I climbed out of my car to find my way inside the doctor's office. Stopping at the entrance, I noticed a closed sign on the door. The fuck? Keyona couldn't be in there if it was closed. So, where was she?

Swaggering back to the car, I shut the passenger door and got back in on the driver's side. I noticed my phone on the floor and snatched it up. I had several missed calls from my mom, Pops, Liz, Lah, and Isi. What was that about?

Disregarding their calls, I made a mental note to hit them back in a few. My main concern right now was Keyona. I woke up with a massive headache and my girl wasn't around. Something was off.

"Hello," I panicked when I heard Keyona's voice. My heart skipped a beat and I was breathing easier. Now, I was ready to light her ass up with questions.

"Baby, where are—"

"Sike! It's the voicemail, bitches! Leave a message. No, don't leave a message actually!"

It was her corny ass voicemail. Man, I told her to change that shit a long time ago. It threw people off. Since Keyona didn't have a job and didn't plan on getting one, she didn't see a need. I would've left a message, but she doesn't check them shits. What's the point of setting up your voicemail if you not going to listen to them? *Bored ass!*

I was pissed more than anything. I had missed calls from everybody except the muthafucka who was missing. Did something bad happen to her? Did she get kidnapped or what? Why wasn't she there when her man woke up? Why was I laid out in the car? Not to mention, none of her shit was here either. Her purse was gone. No trace of a phone or sunglasses. Even her scent was missing.

As I started the car, I was about to head home. "Maybe

she at home, waiting for me to get there," I thought out loud. Feeling my phone vibrate against my thigh, I hit the talk button without looking. I was busy pulling into traffic.

"Hello? Rell??" I was a little surprised to hear Rizz on my line. I might've been confused as to where my fiancée went, but I knew for a fact that Rizz hadn't been fucking with me.

The last time we'd been in each other's space, she told her goof ass boyfriend I was 'their brother'. She didn't tell him we were best friends. What kind of petty shit was that? I won't lie though, hearing her voice on my line was like a breath of fresh air.

"Aye, what's up?" I nonchalantly answered. Yeah, I was salty for the way she'd been shrugging me off. I wasn't one of them lame niggas who didn't show emotion. If I was upset, best believe I was going to make it known.

"Rell, where have you been? Everybody is worried sick about you!" she fussed, sounding truly concerned. Her voice was shaky, and she was gasping in the receiver.

"Everybody?" I kept the same tone. I wanted to see where her head was at.

I knew my mom, pops, sister, and brothers were worried. Rizz hadn't been acting like she cared about me. After that day I kicked her out the car, she was acting like I didn't exist. I hated the shit. I could honestly say I missed the fuck out of my best friend. We'd taken it to another level by having sex. Still, I wanted her to remain my best friend. The line got silent for a moment, then she started talking again.

"Yes, we all been wondering about you. I'm happy you finally answered the phone. Now I can tell everybody you're good."

3

I was about to say something until I heard her dude in the background. "Aye, baby. Who you on the phone with?"

"Nobody." she answered back in an annoyed tone. "But yeah, Rell I miss—"

Click!

I hung up on her. I didn't care to hear shit else she had to say. I was *nobody* to her when her nigga was around. Or, *their brother*. Fuck that.

Just as I was setting my phone back down, it was ringing again. This time, I glanced at the screen. It was my mom. I couldn't intentionally ignore this lady if I wanted to. Not only her, but Pops would beat my ass.

"Yeah, Ma." I blew out a breath. I was becoming real annoyed by everybody blowing my shit up. I just wanted to find my fiancée. She was missing in action and not answering the phone.

"Israel Perez Casique! We've been worried sick about you. Where have you been? Are you okay? Liz said she was on the phone with you and the line just went dead. We've been calling since then. Where have you been?! We've been worried sick about you!" she ranted, repeating different sentences and questions. I knew she was pissed for real. Whenever she got heated, she repeated herself. It was crazy because she didn't know she was doing it.

"Ma, I'm sorry. I can't even tell you what happened. One minute, I'm at the doctor's office with Keyona and the next, I'm waking up in my whip with a headache."

"Where's that bitch?" Ma asked angrily. She didn't like Keyona and never held her tongue about it. It made no difference how many times I asked her to be nice. My mama wasn't for it. She refused to sit in Keyona's face and play nice. Still, she respected my decision to stay with her.

"Ma, that's another thing. I don't know. I'm worried as hell about her. Like, what if someone knocked my ass out and snatched her?" It stressed me to think like that.

Even though Keyona pissed me off half the time, I loved this girl more than anything. She was a little rough around the edges and hard to deal with sometimes. Nevertheless, I didn't want to see anything bad happen to her.

"Rell, are you serious? You wake up and she's nowhere in sight. I mean, how stupid can you be?!" Ma yelled in my ear.

"What you getting at, Ma?" I scratched my head. It was still a little sore. There was a small bump on the back of my head too. Thankfully, there was no blood.

"That bitch knocked you out!" she responded in annoyance.

"What?"

"I'm not about to repeat what you heard. Come to the mansion," she demanded with haste.

"Ma—"

"I don't want to hear it, Rell. Come to the mansion. I need to see your face. I want to be sure you're okay," she calmly stated. I knew when she was calm about her request, she meant business. Ma didn't flip out on the regular. She was cool, collected, and bossy. That's where Lah got that shit from. He rarely raised his voice to get anything across, unless we were all together and no one could hear him. That was Ma through and through. Isi was Pops, but with a side of nice. Liz was off the chain too. She wasn't so out there with hers, though.

"Aight, Ma," I agreed. I still had Keyona on my brain.

However, I couldn't disobey my mother. At the end of the day, it was *Us Before Anything*. I would just have to look for Keyona after this.

Once I arrived at the mansion, I was bombarded with a thousand questions. Everyone except Liz was there. Even Rizz and Kori were in attendance. I peeped Kori sitting on Lah's lap and smirked. That lying nigga. For some reason, I was hoping to see Rizz's nigga hanging around. I didn't see him, though, so it was whatever.

"I promise y'all, I'm good. I just have a small bump on the back of my head. That's it, I swear."

"Well, I'm happy you're here. I want you to stay here tonight—"

"Ma, no," I cut her off. I loved my mother, but she was going about this the wrong way. I knew she was worried about me, but I was good. All I wanted right now was to find Keyona and make sure my seed was good. That's it, that's all.

"Don't fight your mama, son," Pops jumped to the rescue.

"Pops, I get it. Y'all was worried. I'm good now. I have to find Keyona. Is her missing not bothering anyone but me?!" I snapped.

Silence.

Everyone looked around from one to another. I looked them all in the face and nodded my head.

"Wow, y'all fucked up. I know y'all hate her and shit, but she could be dead. Do my feelings for her not mean a damn thing to y'all?!"

Silence.

Still, nobody said anything. I nodded, slowly looking everyone dead in the face. My family wasn't shit right now. They didn't have to care for Keyona. Having a little heart for her wasn't going to hurt them none. They swore Keyona didn't put in any effort, but they didn't either. They would always make a big fuss about if Keyona loved me, she'd try harder. The same shit went for them. They obviously didn't love me enough to put up with her.

"Wow…some family, yo. What's all that shit y'all be spitting about *Us Before Anything*? Huh?! Bullshit! It only works on your own terms!"

"Rell—"

"No! I don't want to hear it!" I was so mad, I didn't know, nor did I care who I was talking to.

Whap!

It was Ma who slapped me. I bucked at her out of reflex. The next thing I knew, I had Isi, Lah, and Pops on my ass. I noticed Kori picking herself up off the floor. Lah must've gotten up so fast, he dropped her.

Ma walked up to me while my brothers and Pops held me down. I knew these niggas were mad because of the way they were breathing. It was all hard and shit.

"You listen to me, and hear me good, Israel!" Ma pointed in my face.

I was struggling to calm down. I was glaring at Ma like she was the enemy and breathing hot and hard as a dragon. The harder I breathed, the more Pops, Isi, and Lah pressed the places they had me pinned by. Pops had me by the neck, making it hard for me to breathe. Isi was squeezing me in a bear hug. This nigga Lah had a whole gun to my head. His crazy ass wasn't afraid to pull the trigger either. About Ma, we didn't play. Any nigga or bitch could get it, fam or not.

Ma licked her lips before she proceeded to say the next thing. "I'm going to let that disrespectful shit go for now. We get that you're upset about your bitch. That's how we raised you. To love and protect who you love! I told you already on the phone how I felt. So, hell no I'm not looking for that bitch. She knocked your ass out, Rell! We all know it! Why can't you see it? Y'all were perfectly fine before all that shit popped off. Then suddenly, you wake up with a knot on the back of your head and don't know shit? Look, I can't tell you why she would've hit you, but she did it. Ain't no way y'all the only ones in the car and you wake up alone. You would've saw it coming. Why you didn't see her coming and knock her ass back is beyond me. I know you extra concerned and all, but here's what you're going to do. You going to wait until she hits you back—"

I began to shake my head no, or at least try. Pops was making it impossible with his firm grip.

"Yes, you are. Listen to me, Rell. I know how shady bitches move. Now, you're going to wait until she calls you back. If she's not calling tonight or morning, something is up. It ain't no fucking kidnapping. That bitch hit you and ran off. What could she be running from? Do you remember anything? What were y'all at the doctor's office for anyway? Let him go, y'all, shit! If I thought he was going to do something, he'd be laid the fuck out by now. Y'all choking my baby!"

Lah, Isi, and Pops obeyed Ma and let me go. She walked up on me as I fell back on the couch and caught my breath. It wasn't like Pops was choking me that much. Feeling my full air flow had me breathing better, though.

Ma grabbed my face and stared into my eyes. "Answer me, Israel. What were y'all doing at that doctor's office?"

This is where I got nervous. The way her eyes were boring into mine, it was as if she already knew the answer.

"Keyona is pregnant…" Hanging my head, I confessed. Ma released my face and took a step back. I was afraid of the look on her face. I knew it wasn't going to be happiness.

Finally looking up, my eyes fell on Rizz, of all people. It was crazy because I was more afraid of what she'd think than anyone. I knew it was because we had sex and copped feelings. Not only that, I hadn't told her anything about it. If I told anybody anything, it was always her first.

Rizz was my confidant. It'd been like that since we were kids. She told me shit, and I did the same with her. We would give each other advice on whatever it was. Half the time, I used her advice. Rizz packed a lot of knowledge. However, I liked to try shit out on my own. Whenever I did that, I'd end up running back to her, saying how much I should've trusted her or took her advice.

Whap!

Ma slapped me again. This time, she didn't stand there and give me some speech. Nor did I buck at her. A nigga was going to be bruised up in the morning. I knew it.

The family room was dead quiet as everyone was in their own thoughts. I peeped the time on my phone. It'd gotten hell of late, just that fast. I lived all the way on the other side of town. Ma and Pops stayed in the boonies.

They lived in this nice ass secluded area just outside of Chicago. It'd take me at least forty-five minutes to get home. I guess I was staying after all. All of us, for that matter. None of us lived close to Ma and Pops. We lived closer to the city. There wasn't even a Walmart out here. They had to drive like thirty to forty-five minutes to get out there too.

My plan was to go home and see if that's where Keyona was. Ma's words sunk in my head for a minute. After giving it some thought, I shook my head. There ain't no fucking way my bitch did me like that. Keyona wouldn't do that.

All I could remember was fighting about her not wanting to go to the doctor's. She was pissed, but I didn't care. I wanted to see what was up with my shorty.

I remembered getting on the phone with Liz. I just couldn't think of what exactly we talked about. Speaking of my baby sis, she wasn't here.

"Where is Liz?" I asked out loud. No one said anything. They barely looked my way. It was like they were treating me like an outsider or some shit. I knew the Keyona being pregnant shit was going to throw them off, but damn. "So, y'all niggas deaf now?"

Good thing Pops wasn't in the room. He would've snatched my ass by the neck again. Isi and Lah still didn't look my way. Rizz was looking at the floor. Now, I was wondering what was on her mind.

Finally, Kori cleared her throat. "Liz is at school. She has classes un—"

"Don't speak to this disrespectful nigga, baby. Matter of fact, come on." Lah grabbed her hand and escorted her upstairs. She looked to me and mouthed the words, *I'm sorry*. I liked Kori. She was cool people. She had her work cut out with Lah's crazy ass, though.

"Come on, baby. Let's go take a bath." Isi pulled Yanna

along. She looked my way with compassion. I knew she was having mixed emotions about everything.

Last and never least, Rizz was left sitting there. She kept her head down, staring at the floor. Honestly, I didn't know what to say to her.

"So, I guess you ain't fucking with me either, huh?" I took a chance and said.

"Never said that…" she lowly replied.

"What?" I was high-key shocked she even spoke to me. Sure, she talked to me on the phone. That was different, though.

"I'm not mad at you, Rell. You were out of line for how you came at Ma, though. If anybody is upset, it's because of that. You need to apologize, for real." She kept it real with me. That's what I loved about her most. Rizz never drew back when it came to telling me shit. I could cop an attitude, but she was going to stay keeping it real.

"You right…" I nodded, looking away.

Never in life did I ever feel more disconnected from Rizz than I did now. Not even when I pushed her away after getting with Keyona. Shit was sad as fuck, bruh. I didn't even know what to say to her right now.

"I know." Her cocky ass had a smile in her voice. Finally, she looked up. She smiled at me. I couldn't resist the urge to get up and hug her. The feeling must've been mutual because she ran to me too.

Meeting in the middle, we tightly embraced one another. "I miss you, Relly."

"I miss you more, Rizzy," I admitted, hugging her tighter.

"No, I do," she argued.

"Nah, I do."

"Nope, I do." She giggled.

"Shut up," I laughed.

"Mhm, cus your ass knows I do." She just wouldn't give it up.

"Irky ass." I ended up squeezing her booty. She swatted my hands away.

"See, now you just doing too much." She pushed me away, rolling her eyes at the same time. "How you going to be crying over Keyona, then turn around and try to push up on me, Rell? Like, really? Just because we talking again, doesn't mean—"

Shutting her up, I snatched her around the waist and pressed my lips on hers. For a small second, she was stiff, fighting against me. I pushed further and slid my tongue in her mouth. She reluctantly accepted it. She let a moan escape and cupped her hands around my face. She ran her fingers along my beard, playing in it.

We were so wrapped up in each other, we didn't hear Liz walk in until she said something.

"Get a room!" she chuckled.

Rizz jumped in her stance and slapped me. I glared at her ass. I had a right mind to slap her ass back. That would only lead to a recap of what happened earlier.

"The fuck you slap me for?" I squinted my eyes.

"Watch it, Rell. You wouldn't want what happened earlier to happen again," Rizz taunted me with a raised eyebrow.

"Fuck you," I snarled at her. She winked and smooched at me before strutting upstairs. I was going to get her ass back.

"Where the hell have you been? What happened earlier?" Liz fired each question at me with a scowl. "I thought something bad happened to you or something. Why didn't you call back?"

"I'm sorry, baby sis. Some shit came up. I got tied up. How was school?" I changed the subject. Liz stood there with squinted eyes for a minute. She was trying to read me.

There was no way I'd tell her Keyona was pregnant. She wouldn't forgive my ass for nothing. Out of everybody, she was the main person rooting for Rizz and I. That wasn't happening no time soon, though.

"What were you trying to tell me on the phone, though?"

"Rell, look, I looked into the shit. My dude got back to me while I was in class. I got the pics and shit…" She took a deep breath.

"Okay, show me." I shrugged.

"Nah, I'm going to show everybody in the morning. I mean, I haven't even looked yet. I'm afraid of what I might see. Which is why we need to do this as a family. Once we all up, we'll talk about how we going about this shit. For now, get some rest big bro. I love you."

"I love you too, lil mama…"

Watching Liz walk away, I wondered what was on those pictures. For now, I'd have to wait. In the pit of my stomach, something was telling me this wasn't going to be good.

CHAPTER 2
PARIS "RIZZ" DANIELS

S tanding in the shower, I allowed the hot beads of teardrop-sized water to peck at my skin. I was thinking about the predicament I was in. I had strong feelings for two different men.

How did I allow my life to spiral like this? Why did I allow myself to fall for both of these men to begin with? Especially knowing only one of them stood a chance at being in my life. Neither Sean nor Rell would be fine with me being cool with the other.

So, what do you do, Paris? is what I've been asking myself over and over these past few days. Do I choose Sean, the man I just met and want to keep getting to know? Or do I choose Rell, the man I've been in love with since we were kids—my best friend?

Sean was new. He was fresh for me. The way I was falling for him had me all excited, like a little school chick with a crush. At first, I wasn't feeling him like that. He was kind of corny. If there was one thing I couldn't stand, it was a corny nigga.

Sean was corny in a cute way, though. He told lame jokes too. I'd laugh each time to make him feel better. He brought out a different side of me. A side I hadn't been in touch with since…well, never. It was like a free side, like I was the only girl. If anything, I guess that's what made me want to keep Sean around. He was interested in only me. He didn't come with baggage like a crazy baby mother, a shady ex, or bad credit.

While he was corny at times, he also seemed to have a little savage in him. He could handle me. He was assertive when need be, but all-around loving.

That's another thing that drew me to him. I was attracted to men who could handle business in and outside the bedroom. Sean and I hadn't had full blown sex yet. I did let him taste my goods, though. When he tried to take it to the next step, I froze up. I wouldn't allow him to enter me. Not after the mind-blowing sex I'd had with Rell, anyway. In some ways, I felt like I was cheating on him. He wasn't even my man, but I felt committed to him. My body was his, until it wasn't.

I've been in love with Rell since we were kids. At one point, I imagined us being more than just friends. Everybody thought that I was blind to our connection. That wasn't the case. I saw it clearly. Hell, I even felt it when we were near each other. I wasn't afraid of the truth. I could admit I was fighting it, though. One reason being that Rell wasn't ready for a commitment with me. Even when he thought he was, he still wouldn't be. He was too connected to Keyona. If we were to be together, the thought of him still loving her would always plague me.

Being with Rell came with consequences. We'd be taking a chance at losing our friendship. While I wanted him bad, I couldn't risk that. He was too precious for me to lose.

Knock, Knock.

"Go away, Rell!" I yelled from the adjoining bathroom in the room I was sleeping in. I knew it was him. He was hellbent on us 'talking'. More like fucking.

"It's not Rell. It's Liz, boo," he shot his best impersonation of his sister. I couldn't help but laugh. This clown was deadass dumb.

Wrapping myself in a thick terrycloth towel, I stepped out of the bathroom and into the bedroom. "Boy, if you don't get the fuck from my door."

"But *Rizzzz*, I want to know what's up with you and Rell. You know my ass is nosey!" He kept up his shenanigans. The next voice I heard was really Liz's.

"*I do not sound like that!*" she exclaimed in a higher pitched tone. I also heard a slapping noise. I assumed Liz popped him. Good. Serves his dumb ass right.

"Oww, damn. You and Mama gon' get enough of slapping a nigga around," Rell huffed at her.

"Whatever. Stop trying to creep in my sis room. She don't want your hoe ass!" Liz made her voice sound like she was ready to pop off ratchetlike.

Rell played along, disguising his deep voice. This nigga even added a snap before responding with, "Guh boo. That ain't what she said when I was—"

Before he could get the whole sentence out, I swung the door open. Standing there, my weight saturated to one side. I didn't have to make a peep. Everything I wanted to cuss was all in the evil glare I was stabbing him with. Tight-lipped, he shut his ass up for a second. I watched as he licked his sexy lips at me before saying the next thing.

Dammit Rizz, don't be a punk for this nigga, I coached myself, keeping a fixed glare.

"Can we talk?" he asked me with sad eyes.

Ugh, I hated that I was a sucker for his ol' uglass! He knew just how to look at me and what to say. No matter how many times I told myself not to feed into it, I did.

Rell was the farthest thing from ugly. His light, caramel skin and juicy dark pink lips made me think about Chris Brown's fine ass. I never stood a chance under the watch of his medium-dark brown bedroom eyes. It was crazy. I'd try and focus my attention elsewhere. His eyes were like two powerful vacuums. They always sucked me in.

What I loved the most was, and it might sound weird, his little-big ass peanut head. When we were kids, I used to tease him for it. In reality, I adored it.

Rell's smile was everything too. It was so straight, white, and pretty. He took good care of his teeth. That was another thing I looked for in a man. Sean had a gap, but I found it kind of cute. Shit, that gap won me over the day he sucked and licked my clit as it rested perfectly in the middle of it.

With him standing so close to me, I could smell the Jimmy Choo cologne on him. I loved that scent. *Come on Rizz, get your life bitch!* Shifting my weight to the other leg, I placed my hand on my hip. I was trying to keep my composure. The way he was looking and smelling, I wanted to jump this nigga's bones right now.

"We ain't got shit to talk about, Rell. All you want to do is come in and fuck." I thought pointing that out would help in some weird way. It didn't do anything but cause tension between my legs.

He stepped as close as close got. If I wasn't so much

shorter than him, we'd be chest to chest. Instead, we were face to chest. He bent down some, peering into my light brown eyes with his dark ones. His lips were so close, I could've kissed him.

"Let me in and quit playing." He was trying to Debo his way in now. Shit, call me Debbie from down the street. I wasn't backing down on his ass.

"Nah, gon' head Rell. We ain't got nothing to talk—" The next thing I knew, he was picking me up and carrying me into the room. "Rell, put me down! I'm not about to play with your stupid ass!"

I was clawing and punching him in the back as hard as I could. I'm sure my nails felt like harmless little darts bouncing off his skin. Next, he tossed me onto the bed.

"Ain't nobody playing but you, ma."

I was now looking up at him like he was crazy. My words were stuck in the back of my throat. I wasn't the one playing. He started all this shit, with his confused ass. I was fine having unspoken feelings from a distance. I was cool with pretending I didn't see the chemistry between us. I could've gone a little longer with keeping my feelings at bay. At least it would've kept the bullshit away.

"Sooo…y'all fucking or what?" Liz sang from the other side of the door. I almost didn't understand her. She started moving her hips back and forth, like she was hitting it from the back. This clown!

I honestly forgot she was standing there. Anytime I was around Rell, it didn't matter who else was in the room. I only saw his ass. I'd start off trying to ignore that he was there, especially when he was with his bitch. It was never easy, though.

"Beat it, blocker." He went to close and lock the door

on Liz. Seizing this moment, I scooted off the big bed and took off running toward the bathroom.

Rell saw me just as he was turning around. He was on my heels but was too late as I slammed the bathroom door and locked it in his face. He punched the door, blowing out a grunt.

"Paris, open this fucking door or else I'll kick the shit in!" He sounded serious as hell. I didn't doubt he'd make good on his threat. I also wanted to see if he'd really kick a door in Kayla Casique's house.

"Do what you got to do, bruh. See if you don't get your ass beat the fuck up," I taunted from my side.

Ms. Kayla wasn't going to play with him for too much longer. After him bucking at her and then admitting Keyona was pregnant? Nah, all it took was one more *tiny* straw and Ma's back would break.

"Man, I don't care about none of that. I just want to talk to you! Why you got to give a nigga a hard time?!" Roughly, he slammed his body against the door.

Jumping back a bit, I clutched my imaginary pearls. This sort of reminded me of when Jody was trying to get into Yvette's apartment after hitting her in *Baby Boy*.

"Why should I let you in? Huh?" I crossed my arms over my chest, thinking, *because I want to see my son*.

"Because I want to see you, Rizzy. We need to talk. I miss you. I love you so much, girl. Just. Open. Up." He might as well have been crying like Trey Songz in a music video. If he didn't get his Tank 'Please Don't Go' ass the fuck from this door…

Blowing out a breath, I rubbed my temple. *This tew much*, I thought as I took a seat on the toilet. "Rell, I love you too, okay? You're my best friend—"

"I ain't talking about that type of love. I love you more than that. I love you like I want you to be my wife. I want to spend the rest of my life, getting old with you. You're it for me, Rizz. You always have been it for me. I was too blinded to see that before. I was too afraid of the outcome of taking that chance with you. I'm ready now. Just open the door, baby, please."

Stuck, I was frozen in a sitting position. *Did this nigga... he did.* While I wanted to open this door and fall into his arms like putty, I was pissed. I couldn't contain the anger building up inside of me. I never felt myself get up, nor did I feel myself snatching the door open. It wasn't until I slapped him that I came to.

"Fuck you, Rell. I waited over twenty years to hear you say that. Now, you got a pregnant bitch—no, *fiancé*! You only want me on your own time. When shit is convenient for you! I've wanted you since I could remember. Now, you want to pull this shit when life isn't going well for you. That's a *fuck you, Rizz*, to my face. So, fuck you too, Rell!"

The look on his face spoke volumes. He wanted to break his foot off into my ass for slapping him. He also wanted to grab me up, kiss me, and hold me like he'd never see me again. I was so irritated with him. I didn't care about the sad look on his face. Nor did I care about the lone tear rolling down his face.

"Get out my face, Rell." I turned my head to look away from him. I couldn't stomach or stand to be around him right now. Even his scent was a sudden turn off.

"Ri—" Of course, he tried to talk to me, but I wasn't trying to hear it.

"Get. Out. My. Face, Rell!" I spat between gritted teeth this time.

When his bottom lip twitched, I knew he wanted to say something else. Instead, he slowly nodded and walked away. A part of me wanted to call out to him. I wanted to stop him. Hug him, kiss him, never let him go—ever. I wanted to say *let's be together* and everything would be alright. Once upon a time, that would've been me.

The other side was saying, *hell no Rizz. Let that nigga go. He don't deserve you! All this time you been waiting for him to say that and he say it now? Fuck no!*

It was a push and pull thing for me. I wanted Israel Perez Casique like sinners in hell wanted water. Then again, Rell was my best friend. Sure, we'd already taken it farther than that.

I can't lie. The shit felt right. I couldn't ignore my feelings for him much longer. Ugh, this can't be life!

Sitting in the Jacuzzi jet springs bathtub, Yanna sat with her back resting against my front. Her head rested perfectly against my broad shoulder. Planting soft, yet firm kisses along her neck, I enjoyed the feel of her big and soft derrière resting on my manhood. My mans was getting excited with her sitting so close. That was anytime my wife was close. I couldn't help it.

Even though it'd been six weeks, I was still a little nervous about making love to her. She hadn't brought it up either. I didn't know where her head was at as far as the miscarriage. She seemed to bounce back from it, though.

She kept a smile on her face, which kept me in good spirits. Especially during the times I was feeling down. After the loss of our child, I felt empty. I hadn't even met him or her.

I can't lie. I blamed myself. I felt like maybe if I just stopped that night, maybe we would be having a baby now. Yanna saw things differently, though. She was so encouraging and strong. I mean, we both suffered a loss, yet she went through the physical pain and managed to keep a smile.

While she hadn't spoken too much about the miscarriage lately, she'd been talking about us having another baby. I wasn't against it, but I wasn't in the right headspace to be for it. Yanna asked me where all my faith had gone. It was still there. Just a little distant. I missed my child and didn't even know them. Ain't that fucked up?

"Baby?" Yanna called out to me, bringing me out of my thoughts.

"Yeah, babe?" Moving her hair out the way, I kissed her shoulder and the nape of her neck.

"I've been thinking a lot lately…" She turned slightly to look me in the eyes. I made eye contact, giving her my undivided attention.

"What's on your mind?"

She pulled her bottom lip into her mouth, biting it before saying, "I want us to try IVF."

"IV who?" I asked, scrunching up my face.

She giggled before repeating herself. "IVF, babe."

"What's that?" I quizzed. I'd honestly never heard of it.

"It's when you want to have a baby and can't conceive on your own. So, you have someone else carry your baby." she explained, staring in my eye the entire time. The glimmer of hope dancing in her eyes told me she'd been considering this more than a few days.

"So, you mean like me getting someone else pregnant?" My face was still twisted up with my nostrils flaring. If she said yes, I'd say hell no. Wasn't no female but Yanna carrying my children. I meant that shit. If she couldn't carry my babies, we'd just adopt a few kids and get us a puppy.

"No, the egg comes from me. The doctor just mixes it in a tube with your sperm. Then, they insert it inside an eligible female, and she carries the baby to term. She has our baby and then gives it to us." Yanna turned back around, using her hands to explain like it was that simple.

Shaking my head, I hated to disagree with my wife, but shit, it was life. "Nah, boo I'm not feeling that. I mean, having another woman and not you carrying our baby? There's too many technicalities with that, ma."

Slightly, she turned back to look at me. I didn't miss the identical irritation in her voice and face. "Like?"

"Like, what if the bitch run off with our baby because she decides she want the baby for herself? What if she miscarries too? What if—"

"Heard you." Yanna pulled herself from the water and stood. Bending over, she had her ass in my face as she pulled the plug out the tub. As the water began to drain, I stood and stepped out behind her. She transferred to the stand-up shower.

Stepping into the shower behind her, I rinsed myself off too. After rinsing in silence, we went into the room and dried off. The strain between us was so thick, you could slice it with a knife. I knew it was due to Yanna being upset. Not that I didn't care, because I did. I meant what I said about the IVF thing, though. Wasn't no other bitch carrying my seeds, and that's that.

I mean, she didn't even give us a chance to try and have another baby on our own. Her having endometritis was a load of bullshit to me. Those doctors didn't know what they were talking about. If it was as bad as they claimed, how did she end up pregnant to begin with?

Yanna slipped one of my shirts and boxers on and climbed into bed. She was all the way on one side of the bed with her back turned to me. I wasn't feeling that shit at all. After drying off, I slid into bed. Scooting to the middle, I pulled her into me.

"Stoop, Isi! I'm not in the mood," she whined, swatting my hands away.

"Aye, aye, aye. Cut that shit out." I snatched one of her ass cheeks. "Since when do we go to bed mad at each other?"

"N—"

"Not never, nigga." I mocked Kat Williams voice. She started laughing loudly.

"Ughh! I can't stand your uglass! Still, go away. I'm mad at you right now." She nudged me in the abdomen.

"But you love me, mama. Your ass ain't mad. Shut up." I kissed her on the nape of her neck.

"I do love you. But I want to do the IVF, baby," she huffed in a pout. She only pouted when she couldn't get her way. Any other time, I gave in. That was only due to the situations being minor. This wasn't that. This something that took an incredible amount of research and thinking. You don't just hand of your child to someone without thinking first.

"I heard you, mama. I'm not feeling that too much. I told I—"

"You're thinking negative about the whole thing, babe. Maybe if you should look more into it," she whined, still trying her hand at convincing me.

"What happened to all that faith you had in us having

26

our own baby, huh? Just like two weeks ago, you were all hyped about trying again. You was like, *fuck them doctors. I'm gon do me!*" I did my best to mimic her.

She was back to laughing all hard and shit. "Yeah, I want to try and have our own baby too. If that doesn't work—"

"It's going to work." I cut her off before she could explain further.

"But baby—"

"But nothing, babe. It's going to work. Say it." I pinched the same cheek I had a tight grasp on. She was about to protest, but I pinched harder.

"Oww, Isiah!"

"Say it."

"It's going to work," she dryly stated. I pinched her again.

"Say it with passion," I demanded.

"It's going to work. Now, let go of my ass so I can go to sleep."

"Nah, give me them lips first." I kept the same demanding tone. She turned and put her lips against mine. I stole the moment, sliding my tongue and sucking her bottom lip. "Thanks, but I was talking about the southern set."

"Well, why didn't you just say so?" Smiling deviously, she kissed my lips more.

Gently, I pulled her on top of me. Pulling myself into a sitting position, it allowed my wife to straddle me. Staring into her beautiful brown eyes, I still saw my whole world. That alone threw a shock wave through my body.

Pulling the shirt over her head, her breasts were exposed. Hungrily, I eyed them like my last meal. Taking the left nipple into my mouth, I carefully massaged her right breast. Yanna began to moan and grind against me. Her nipples were her spot.

Feeling her bare pussy rub against my exposed manhood, I became hard. Lifting up some, Yanna stroked my shaft into fullness. She then positioned herself to where the head of my dick was at her opening.

Slowly sliding down, we both let out an overdue growl. She was so warm, wet, and tight. I didn't want to say I forgot what she felt like, but six weeks was a long ass time! Especially when you were used to getting it on a daily.

"Mmm, babe..." she cooed as she slowly began to ride me. My hands reached for her soft ass cheeks like a magnetic force. I squeezed them and pulled them apart, guiding her up and down my dick.

"Gotdamn...baby, you feel good as fuck," I complimented her, biting my bottom lip. I wasn't trying to be too loud. After all, we were in my parent's house.

"Don't hold back, baby. Give it to me harder..." she begged in my ear. As much as I wanted to follow her request, I was scared. The last time I went too hard, we lost our baby.

"Shit, baby, slow down," I whispered, my head buried deep in her neck. Between the pace she was going and her scent, I was becoming harder. I didn't think it was possible to become harder than I already was. It was like my dick was full of built-up nut and needed to be freed.

"Nooo, baby. I need to feel you deeper inside of me!" she shrieked out, riding me faster and harder. I tried to slow her pace down by squeezing her ass and taking control. That only made her go harder than before.

"Fuuuck, mama! Do it just. Like. That…" I couldn't do shit but let her do her. Apparently, my baby needed to be fucked hard. Who was I to deny her that? Leaning back, I let her take full control.

Other than the little light shining into the room by the moon, the room was completely dark. Still, I could see her face all twisted up. I could see her biting and sucking her bottom lip and her eyes rolling to the whites.

I wasn't expecting us to have a full love making session. I just wanted to eat her pussy until she was begging me to stop. Even then, I wouldn't stop until she was in a deep slumber. I wanted to feel my wife's southern lips glide over my lips and taste her sweetness riding my face. That was it.

"Isi…I want to cum, daddy. I want to cum!" she moaned out in a begging manner. Shit, I was ready to bust too!

Flipping her onto her back, I hovered over her naked body. Yanna was gasping for air while begging me to finish fucking her. Into the dark, guided by moonlight, I stared down at her beautiful face. I watched how her mouth hung open as I slowly pressed each inch into her.

Once I was deep enough, I began to give her slow strokes. I did this until she begged me to go deeper and a little faster. Picking up the pace, I gave my queen what she wanted.

"I love you, Isiah. ILoveYou. ILoveYou. ILoveYouuu!" she sang out. She didn't have to tell me that she'd cum. I felt it happen. It didn't take long for me to do the same.

"I love you, baby." I gave her a few kisses on the lips.

I was about to pull out and cuddle up with her. She stopped me, locking her legs around my waist. She began rotating her hips underneath me, moaning breathlessly. "Nooo…stay here."

Just like that, I rocked up and continued making love to my wife.

❦

The next morning, everybody was dragging, one by one, into the kitchen. From the looks of it, we all had gotten some cutty last night. Well, everybody except Rell and Rizz.

Everybody but them was all full of smiles, giggles, dancing, spinning around and shit. It was like we were in the *High School Musical* music video *"We're All In This Together."* Even Liz had a little groove going on for herself. Now, I was wondering if she'd snuck Shanah in last night. They'd been kicking it pretty heavy since they met.

Rell and Rizz, I didn't know what was up with them. Whatever it was, had them in a little funk. Both wore deep scowls. They couldn't be a part of the music video. That was cool, though. They could keep their negative energy to themselves.

"Good morning everybody!" Kori came bouncing into the room with a huge smile on her face. She could be in the music video. She was happy too.

"Good morning!" everyone that was a part of the music video spoke. We even answered in unison, like we were singing the same tune. Next, Lah came into the room all smiles and shit. I smiled, nodding and silently welcoming him into the music video.

"Today I begin a new life. For I am the master of my abilities

and today is going to be a great and beautiful day." He quoted *Jody 10:18.*

"This nigga!" I couldn't contain my laughter.

"Awl hell. Nasty!" Rizz threw a piece of her bagel at him with a screw face. "Boy, sit your uglass down."

"I guess somebody ain't get no cutty last night. Huh, baby?" Lah leaned down and kissed Kori in the mouth.

I had to blink my eyes twice, making sure I was seeing that right. Lah didn't do shit like that, let alone bring anybody with him to the mansion. I could say Kori was different because she was like family. She was Lah's girl, and he just openly proved it by kissing her in front of all of us. Smiling goofily, Kori was giggling like a fool.

"I guess not." She winked at Rizz. Rizz smirked at her cousin.

Ma walked into the kitchen next, her heels making noise as they connected with the hardwood floors. *"Terms of endearment? Public affection? Today's a new day?* Aww! What's next?"

"Allow me to introduce the future Mrs. Islah Perez Casique." I laughed, adding my two cents. Lah glanced my way so fast the nigga could've gotten whiplash. I winked at him. He squinted his eyes at me.

"Stop it, Isiah. Leave your brother alone." Ma snickered, taking a sip of her coffee. "But real shit. *When's the wedding?*"

"See!" I pointed at Ma. She started cracking up, damn near choking on her first sip. I kept up with my antics, humming the wedding song. "Dun, dun, dun-dun!"

"Y'all are too much this morning." Yanna joined the laughter as she placed a plate with eggs, bacon, pancakes and a glass of apple juice in front of me. In return, I gave her a tight squeeze on the booty. She giggled, swatting my hands away.

"Stop being nasty."

"Like you were last night—well, this morning?" I whispered in her ear as a reminder. She couldn't stop giggling to save her life.

Whap!

"Nasty pendejo!" I was caught off-guard by Mama. She came into the kitchen in a powder blue bathrobe and matching house slippers. In between her thumb and index finger appeared to be a lit cigarette. However, it smelled like cannabis.

"Oww, damn Grandma!" I rubbed the spot she slapped. Yanna rubbed and kissed it for me.

"Oh, shut up! I didn't hit you that hard," she fussed at me. "Good morning, my baby," she turned to Yanna, speaking in a loving tone. *Ain't that a bitch?*

"Good morning, Mama."

"Aye, Mama. Let me hit that cigaweed," Lah said with a mouth full of food.

"Nigga, you ain't put in on this." Mama took a puff. I knew it wasn't an ordinary cigarette. I never got why she packed weed into cigarettes, though.

"Are you supposed to be smoking?" Yanna placed her hand on her hip, shifting her weight with a raised eyebrow.

"No, she's not." Pops came in next. Snatching the cigarette out her hand, he puffed on it himself. Mama glared at him like a dog who just got their steak taken away. "Mama, you know better than this. You've come too far to be puffing these cancer sticks again," Pops scolded her.

"Who died and made you my damn daddy? Kayla, get your nigga before he gets got." She pointed at Ma, who put her hands up and shook her head.

"Damn, baby. You'll let your nigga get got?" Pops looked hurt, looking at Ma.

"If a nigga want to talk to his mama crazy, yup!" Ma's petty ass, I swear. She was directing her comment toward Rell. He was the only one who hadn't spoken.

Despite the little attitude searing off her, Rizz spoke. She was maintaining a smile. I knew different, though. Something was bothering sis.

"Ma, can we talk?" Rell asked Ma. She placed her hand on her hip and cut her eyes at him. The room grew quiet as we all watched between him and ma. We were waiting on her reaction to him.

From the corner of my eye, I saw Mama sneaking out with the cigaweed. Pops had placed it near the microwave. I shook my head but didn't say a word. Mama was something else, man.

"Yeah, come on and talk." Ma nodded to Rell and then walked out. Rell stood to follow her out.

"Is," Pops called out to me. I looked up, making eye contact.

"Pops," I answered him.

"Come meet me in the office for a minute."

Before getting up to go meet with him, I made sure my wife was straight. She let me know that she, Rizz, Liz, and Kori had plans. They were supposed to be having a 'girl's day'.

"What's up with you, Pops?" I took a seat in the chair in front of him.

"Nothing, really. I wanted to touch base with you

about…you know…everything. How are you feeling?" He leaned back in his chair. Deeply sighing, I hung my head and then sat up straight in the chair. I looked my pops in the eyes and weakly smiled.

"Some days are better than others for me. My main concern be Yanna, though. If she good, that's all I care about."

He nodded his head with a smile. "I hear you. That's the thing to do, son. Make sure you take care of home first —always that. Now that home is taken care of, you have to take care of you. You can't carry on like this isn't affecting you. Holding a smile for Yanna is only making you weaker. You have to hold that smile for yourself as well, my boy."

I nodded, hearing his knowledge. Honestly, I'd cried all I could. I wasn't usually one to let things carry on for too long. I liked to do what I had to do and then let it be that. The same thing applied with this situation.

"I hear you. I've cried and all that stuff, Pops. I'm just ready to try to have a baby with my wife now," I explained with a heavy sigh.

It hurt my core to lose my child. I felt fucked up for days—weeks. I could barely be around my wife. It wasn't because I blamed her. It was because I blamed myself. I placed it all on my shoulders.

Twenty-seven was creeping up on me at the end of the month. I always knew I'd be starting or have a little family by now. Shit, I was as ready as ever to start one. This IVF shit Yanna was talking had me bent. I'd adopt a kid before having another woman push my kid out.

Yanna said I needed to look more into it. I would. However, all I heard coming out her mouth was 'another woman having my seeds'. Nope, I wasn't for it—at all! I believe she could get pregnant again. We'd just have to let nature take its course.

"Pops?"

"What's up?"

"You know Yanna wants to have an artificial ba—"

Crash! Boom!

I was cut off by the sound of something falling and breaking. "What the fuck…"

Me and Pops rushed out the den to find the commotion. When we got downstairs, Rell was on the floor in the family room. He was standing next to the glass coffee table. Everything that once sat on it was now on the floor. His face was red, and his eyes were black.

The one thing Pops did pass down to all his kids was that our eyes turned black when we were pissed. It was some creepy shit, but it happened. All of us had dark brown eyes to begin with, so imagine them going from this pretty brown shade to pitch black.

"Bro, what's wrong?" Slowly, I walked up on him.

I noticed Ma and Liz were off to the side. Liz had tears in her eyes. Ma had a mug mean as a pit. Seeing my mother and sister with distorted expressions always fucked me up inside. I was becoming agitated and didn't even know what was bothering them.

"What's wrong, yo?" Lah came rushing down the stairs with Kori on his heels.

Rell held the picture in his hands up. Just as I was about to grab it, he shoved it in my chest with aggression. He was glaring at me like I was the enemy. I glared back before staring down at the photo. My hands shook as I dropped it.

"What the...fuck?" My head was spinning now. There just wasn't any way I was seeing what I was seeing.

"Is, what's up? What's on the photo?" Lah came over to me and snatched the photo off the floor.

He was now glaring at it with disgust. The next thing I knew, he drew his gun and aimed it at me? He was breathing extra hard and everything.

"Islah! Stop! What are you doing? Why are you holding a gun to your brother?!" Kori screamed in a shaky tone. She didn't even know what was going on. I felt bad because she'd just gotten here and was already mixed up in bullshit.

A small tear slid down my face as I stared at my baby brother with a gun held to my chest. If he was going to pull the trigger, he might as well had done it. I knew he wouldn't. He was just mad about what he saw on that paper.

"Stay out of this shit, Kori! It has nothing to do with you." he barked at her. She took a step back and slowly nodded with hurt in her eyes.

"Heard you." She walked out of the room. Lah glance in her direction and then turned back to me.

"It's been you this whole time. You been plotting on the fam and fucking Rell's nigga at the same time," he seethed.

"What?!" Pops roared, glaring in my direction. Yanna was on her way downstairs. She'd heard everything.

"What? Shut up, Islah. You don't know what you're talking about..." She came in and stood next to me. "Isi couldn't have had time to be doing any of that shit you're speaking on."

"Well, maybe you been helping too. Since y'all so close and shit." This nigga aimed the gun to my wife—my rub.

I hauled off and socked his dumb ass in the throat. Once he was down, I kicked the gun away from him. This nigga Lah acted on emotion. Once he regained his breath, he'd surely try and light my ass up like they did Ricky on *Boyz n the Hood*.

"Baby, calm down! There has to be a perfect explanation for this." Yanna grabbed my face.

She hadn't even seen the photo. Therefore, she didn't know what everybody was so heated about. This is why I loved the fuck out this woman. She had my back first. She didn't care what was happening or whatever. She just knew she was riding for her nigga. This was my hitta, for real.

I snatched the picture off the floor and handed it to her. She stared down at it. I watched her face turn in three different directions. The first one was shock, like she couldn't believe what she was seeing. The second was anger. I was a little worried that she might believe what she saw. Last, the third was relief. She didn't believe what she was seeing.

"Y'all, this isn't Isi." She looked around the room. "*Is this what y'all so mad about?*"

Liz had let her tears fall. She nodded and sighed, staring up at the ceiling. I hated to see my baby crying. More than anything, I hated that she lost hope in me. Yanna began to pass the photo around so everybody could see it.

"Thanks, baby," I kissed her lips.

"You know I got you." She kissed me repeatedly. This was my everything. Because of that, I wanted to give her everything. I might've not been with this IVF shit she was speaking about. However, I'd look more into it for her.

"I love you."

"I love you too." She kissed me a few more times.

"If it ain't Isi, who is it then?" Rell was still feeling some type of way. As he should. I'd be pissed too if I found out my bitch was plotting on me with someone who looked exactly like my brother.

The craziest shit was dude did look like me. He appeared to be a bit older than me, though. The only difference was his tats and his eyes. I mean, how could my family not realize the eyes? The same eyes we all shared—dark brown. His were some green color.

The room was so quiet, you could hear the mice in the walls fucking—if there were any. I looked around the room. Ma was grilling Pops hard as fuck. Lah was rubbing his neck. Rell was damn near on the verge of crying.

I watched his chest heave up and down and his nostrils flare. His bottom lip was quivering. He continued to shake his head, trying to avoid the tears that threatened to fall. I could see my bro was trying to hold it together. Before I knew it, we were all catching him before he fell.

Me, Liz, and Lah held him as he roared out obscenities. Too bad Rizz wasn't here for this moment. I didn't recall hearing her leave, but she had to have left. There was just no way she couldn't hear all this commotion.

"Answer your son, Perez. Who is this nigga that looks just like *my* son?" Ma calmly asked. There was a method to Ma. When she yelled, she wasn't all that upset, but when she spoke in a calm tone…that's when you knew. She wasn't on games.

"Kayla…not here, not now." Pops spoke between

gritted teeth, throwing Ma a scowl. I was busy holding my brother, but I wasn't blind. Something was off with them. Dude in the picture had everything to do with it.

"Then when—" Ma started to question, but Pops sharply cut her off.

"Kayla!" he yelled in a hushed tone before gritting his teeth. "Not. Now."

Ma squinted her eyes but didn't speak. She knew better than to get Pops riled up. They had a relationship where everything was versatile. Growing up, I'd seen Pops put Ma out on the couch a few times. I used to think they were just playing. That is, until I'd wake up in the morning, leaving for school and Ma was all z's on the sofa. Mouth all opened and everything.

After ma dismissed herself, Pops stood there for a minute. He then dispersed from the room as well. Now, I wanted to know who dude in the picture was. Other than that, I knew one thing for sure. Keyona was a dead bitch.

Though I was upset it had to be like this, I was also relieved that my brother wouldn't be dealing with her anymore. It was time for him to be happy and do him. I just prayed that his heart healed vastly. He had a good ass woman waiting for him. At least I hoped Rizz waiting.

CHAPTER 4

RELL

Two weeks later…

H *ello? Sike! You reached the voicemail bitches! Leave a message. No, actually, don't leave a message!*

This was my fortieth time getting Keyona's voicemail. I knew she had to have blocked my number or shut her phone off. It'd been two weeks straight already. I had a whole search team after that bitch.

"You still trying to call that bitch, huh?" Lah broke me out my thoughts. I looked to him with the side eyes.

"You're damn straight! You'd be calling Kori if she snaked you and stopped answering your calls," I called his ass out. Fucking around with Lah's ass, he'd probably go gunning for her. "Speaking of which, where is she at? Is she coming to the lake house? Why is she not riding with you instead of me?"

"I don't know. I think she's coming with Rizz. I don't have a GPS on her pussy, damn! You should've been planting one on Keyona's ass. You're riding with me because it's my turn to babysit your suicidal ass."

"Nigga, I ain't suicidal." I smacked my gums. It was Ma's idea to have my siblings watching me around the clock. It went Isi, Liz, and then Lah. I couldn't even go home yet, which pissed me off to the fullest. So, I was either at Isi's or Lah's. Liz watched me when she was home at the mansion. This muthafucka took it to heart and was driving me anywhere but home. You know how many dates I had been on with this wanch and Shanah? Too damn many!

"Nah, I can't call it." He shook his head. "You steady trying to call that nigga, Ken."

"Fuck up, big head boy. As I said, you'd be doing the same."

"Whatever. Then why I'm not doing it now?" He looked at me with his lips pressed to the side.

"I don't know. Why you not hitting her up? That's your lady, bruh. What? She snaked you?"

He waved me off and then cranked the car. "That ain't my lady. She's, my bitch." he corrected me. "And if she snaked me, we wouldn't sitting here right now. We'd be separated by some thick ass glass, using one of them unsanitized pay phones. On Mama, we would."

Next, he flinched, looking out the window and in the backseat. I laughed hella hard. It reminded me of Smokey from the movie *Friday*.

"You tweaking as fuck! Mama ain't here." I called it. Ever since his 'fake gang banging ass' put something on Mama, he'd been tweaking, looking around for her anytime he said it. "The fuck is the difference? She's your lady, nigga."

"Anyway, fuck all that. She may or may not be there. I don't know. She call herself being mad at me. She knows what's up, though." he said, sure of himself.

"Why is she mad?" I pried.

"Damn, why you all over in my mix? You better worry about that nigga Ken."

"Ha-ha. Y'all got all the jokes, huh?" I waved him off, looking out the window.

They could say what they wanted about Keyona. I invested a lot of time in that girl. I was there when nobody else was there for her. It was me who stayed down with her when nobody else was rocking with her. How she go and do me like this? Then, to top it off, she was pregnant by me. If she didn't come out for me, at least for my seed.

"My bad, bro. Real shit, I feel for you. I may not fuck with that bitch, but she's carrying my little niece or nephew. If it means anything, I'm sorry you're going through this shit, and you know I'm here through it. Us before anything, always." He held his fist out to give me dap.

I dapped him up. "Us before anything bro."

An hour later, we pulled up to the lake house. I had some smooth memories at this joint. I used to look forward to coming out this way. It'd been a minute, so being here would bring back old memories. Thank God for my sis, Yanna.

It was her idea to get us all out here. She felt it was long overdue. I agreed with her. Plus, with all the bullshit going on, we all needed this trip. The lake house was located in Indianapolis. It took a little over an hour to get there.

"Aye, Frick and Frack finally here. Why y'all always the

43

last ones to show up to the function?" Rizz came off the porch, looking fine as hell. She was looking hella thick in the white sun dress she was wearing. She was the only woman I knew who looked like everything in white. Her ass looked so big, I wanted to squeeze it. I knew better, though.

This was the first time we'd been around each other since the last time at the house. I can't lie. A nigga's feelings were hurt after she said what she said. She'd been holding back from me for over twenty years. Man, this weekend would be hard to focus on anything.

"Shut up, head ass. Where my bitch at?" Lah's ass asked. Rizz looked him upside the head.

"Umm, nigga, *your who?* Surely not my sister, Kori." She checked him, getting in his space. I put my hand around her waist and pulled her back.

"Y'all chill."

She pushed my hand off her, glaring at me. "You tell his hot ass to chill. Ain't no bitches over here."

After saying that, she strutted away. I was in a daze watching the rotation of her ass cheeks. Pulling my eyes away, I caught Lah staring at her ass with his mouth open. This nasty nigga was pretending to jack off too.

I popped him upside the head. "Get yo nasty ass…"

"Is it me or did Rizz's booty get bigger?" he scratched the top of his head.

"Her booty always been that big, my nigga. Quit looking at it!" I popped him upside the head. "Kori gon' beat yo ass."

"Man, shut yo sensitive ass up. Kori ain't gon' beat on shit but take this dick when I see her ass." he gloated.

"Didn't you just say she wasn't fucking with you?"

"She hasn't been this last week. I think I hurt her feelings or some shit. I don't know." He shrugged.

"The fuck? Nigga." I palmed my face and shook my head. "How you don't know? If she ain't fucking with you, you've hurt her damn feelings, man."

"Okay, so what do I do?" he asked in desperation. I smirked some. "This shit ain't funny, Rell. I really don't know what to do. I'm new to this shit."

I crossed my arms over my chest. This nigga swore he wasn't feeling Kori. Now, look at his asking for advice ass. "You really want to know how to get back on her good side?"

"Yeah, nigga. That's what I said." He nodded with raised eyebrows. Impatient ass. I stalled just to see him squirm a little. I was enjoying this 'big brother tease little brother' moment.

"You have to eat her pussy." I Kanye shrugged after that. Lah stood there, like he was thinking about it. Like what I said was rocket science or some shit. "What?"

"I don't eat pussy. I promised myself I'd wait until I get married for that. Eating pussy is a privilege *only* wifey gets." he explained his logic. While I agreed one hundred percent, I didn't live by that. I'm not saying I go around sticking my tongue in every woman bumping their pussy against my face. I also didn't hold back this lethal tongue power.

"I guess she just gon' be mad then." I was out of advice to help him. Eating Keyona's pussy had gotten me out of *many* arguments. Just then, something hit me. maybe that would work on Rizz too.

"Fuck that. If that's all you got, I guess her ass gon' be

mad until she ready to speak." He huffed, bringing me out of my thoughts.

"Have you reached out to her?" I asked.

"You mean like call or go to her house?" he countered.

Nodding my head, I answered. "Yeah, bro,"

"I went to her house once. She wasn't there. I was going to break in like last time. We had a talk a week ago, and she explained that she wasn't cool with me breaking in. I'm trying to respect her little boundaries, but she's testing me. I called three times one day, and she didn't answer. Matter fact, she sent my ass to voicemail the third time. I haven't called her since then."

"You only called her three times on one day?" I asked, cracking up. This nigga couldn't be serious.

"Tree times nigga, one day. What I say?" he mimicked Birdman's way of saying three. I was in hysterics.

"Well, tree times in one day isn't enough bro. You have to get her attention in another way." I patted him on the shoulder and left him standing in the driveway.

When I walked into the house, the smell of fresh paint and wood attacked my nose. That told me Pops and Ma had some work done to the house. The deeper I walked into the house, I heard voices coming from the kitchen. I knew for a fact Liz and Rizz were here. I remember spotting Isi's Jeep in the driveway. This nigga took it old school. I knew he only brought it because we planned on going camping while we were out here. He had the tents, sleeping bags, and Liz's s'mores ingredients in the back. There were only four tents. Everybody except me and Rizz were boo'd up. Ma and Pops weren't going. They both said hell nah, they weren't cut for it.

"Hey, family!" I walked in and greeted everyone.

"Hey, bro!" Liz and Isi welcomed me first.

Next, Ma walked up to me. "Hey, baby. How are you feeling today?"

"I'm good, Ma. Thanks for asking."

"Of course. I won't have to take your phone this weekend, right?" she asked with a raised eyebrow.

"Nah, I'm good, Ma." I reassured her with a kiss on her cheek.

Every day since finding out Keyona snaked me, Ma had been on me. She made sure I was fed and did everything to keep my mind off the situation. I thought she was doing too much but wouldn't get in the way of her doing her motherly duties. Her wanting another baby crossed my mind. I was starting to think maybe Pops did knock her up on vacation.

"Where is Pops?" I didn't notice him anywhere.

"He's in the office area working on something last minute. He'll be down in a few." Ma rolled her eyes, taking a seat at the table with everyone else. They were all eating sandwiches and chips.

Watching them eat made me hungry. Walking over to the sink, I went to wash my hands to make a sandwich and join everybody. Just then, I was hit by Rizz's favorite body spray from Bath and Body works—Wild Madagascar and Vanilla. I would know because she got it every time we went shopping together. It smelled good on her too.

Turning to see where she was, my eyes narrowed, and my skin became hot when I noticed who she was standing there with. My appetite and mood was shot.

CHAPTER 5

RIZZ

The look on Rell's face was priceless when he turned around and saw me standing in the kitchen entrance with Sean. He was madder than the devil when he wanted to see you fail. In this case, I knew Rell didn't want to see me with Sean. Anybody, for that matter.

"Hey, Rizz!" As always, Yanna, and Liz were the first to speak when I entered the room.

"Hey, babes," I softly smiled, looking at the reaction on Rell and Isi's faces. Rell was sneering while Isi appeared unsure. I knew why Rell was mad. Isi, though, I thought he was cool with Sean.

"What's up, John?" He got up and came to dap Sean up.

"What's up, man. It's Sean, remember?" Sean lightly chuckled. If that didn't piss me off more than anything, I don't know what did.

I hated that Sean would let shit like that slide. He didn't really stand up for himself, and I hated that shit. He needed to put his foot down more often and people

49

wouldn't walk all over him. Even the people at his job walked over him, and he allowed it.

"Oh, yeah, my bad, bro." Isi nodded to him.

"Your what?" There went Sean lightly chuckling again. I rolled my eyes.

"Nothing, bro. Good seeing you again. Rell, you remember John?" Isi turned to Rell's mad ass as he was walking out the kitchen.

"Nope," he nonchalantly spoke.

Just as he was walking out, Lah was coming in. "Sis, who told you it was okay to bring John's ass here?"

I turned around, placing my hand on my hip and shifting my weight. I glared at him. He had me fucked up since he referred to Kori as a bitch. "His name is Sean."

"What's up, man?" Sean's nice ass held his hand out for Lah to shake. I wanted to slap it away. Lah wasn't going to shake him up no way.

Instead of speaking, Lah went into the kitchen and kissed Ms. Kayla. Shaking my head, I palmed my face. I knew this was a bad idea to let Sean come here. I told him to give my family a little more time. He insisted on coming out, though, so I agreed.

"Maybe I should leave." he whispered near my ear.

Geez, ya fucking think, Sherlock? I thought in my mind, rolling my eyes before turning around to face him. "No, you don't have to do that, Sean. Just let me talk to everyone, first."

By *everyone*, I meant Rell. He was the only one with the real issue here. I really did want Sean to stay and meet the people I called my family. I'd invited him, thinking it'd be the perfect ice breaker. Shit was breaking alright. Just not in my favor.

"Yeah, I don't think they're liking me too much, babe. Plus, this is a family holiday. I'll just head back to Illinois and spend the week with my family," he explained with a smile.

Illinois? I thought to myself with a raise to my eyebrow. If he didn't just say *'I'm going back to Chicago'* and call it the damn day… "I really wanted you to stay and get to know my family."

"How about I come back in a couple of days? You said you guys were going camping, right? We could try again then." he suggested. I was getting even more upset.

The more I tried to get him to stay, he was making up excuses to leave. It was like he didn't want to truly get to know me.

They might've been rough around the edges. However, getting to know my family was a part of getting to know me. If he didn't want to do that, we couldn't make anything happen between us.

"I guess…" I ended up shrugging my shoulders. I didn't see the point in trying to convince him. If he wanted to stay, he would.

"Two days, babe. Camping. Promise." He hugged, then kissed me on the forehead. Weakly, I smiled at him to ensure no hard feelings.

"Mkay, see ya." I waved as he got back into his car. I stayed out on the porch until I didn't see his car anymore.

Going back inside the house, Rell was waiting for me in the living room. I wasted no time lighting his ass up. "How could you embarrass me like that?! Sean left because of you!"

He stood there staring with his narrow eyes transfixed on me. "That nigga grown as fuck, ma. If he wanted to stay, he would've. Looks to me he couldn't wait to get his ass out of here."

"Whatever. It's only because of how you made him feel," I argued, sticking up for Sean.

"If he was real, he would've stuck around. A real man doesn't let anything come between what he wants. Makes you wonder if dude really wants you, huh?"

I shoved him in the chest. "Fuck you, Rell!"

He just stood there, not saying another word. I watched as his eyes began to wildly roam my body. He was eyeballing me like I was a big, fat juicy steak. The fact that he wasn't responding to me pissed me off more than anything.

"Why are you looking at me like—" Before I could get another word out, he picked me up in one swift motion. I began to beat on his back and yell. "Put me down, Rell!"

"No," he huffed out, taking the stairs leading to the rooms two at a time.

"Rell, I'm not about to play with your—"

"You're the only one that's playing, Paris." He shut me up with a passionate kiss. It felt so good, so right. Like, this was the hydration I'd been waiting my whole life for.

"Rell…" I moaned between kisses. Then, I realized what was going on. "No! stop! Just…stop it, please!" I pushed him away.

"I love you, Paris. I always have, always will—"

I cut him off with a shove. "Shut up, Israel! You don't love me. If you did, you would do whatever it took to see me happy. You wouldn't stand in the way of it."

"So, I wouldn't make you happy? Say the word, and I promise I'll walk out this room and your life. All I want is you happy. If ol' boy does that for you, say it." He held his arms out like he was in a Silk or TGT music video.

"You're selfish, Rell. That's not fair, and you know it. How are you going to just walk out my life because of Sean? We've been best friends since we were kids. Sean shouldn't come between anything we have going on."

"Anything?" He got closer to me. I pushed him away. He grabbed my arms and pushed me gently against the door. I stared into his eyes as he stared back into mine.

"Rell, this can't happen anymore." I managed to breathe out.

"Why not? You want it just as bad as I do."

Our lips were so close, I could suck his bottom lip into my mouth. "That's the problem."

"What is?" He was kissing along my jaw.

"This. Us, doing this is the problem. We can't do this anymore." I had my eyes closed. I wanted to fight what was happening so bad, but I couldn't. It was like I said. When I was under Rell, I lost all my sense. I was putty in his hands.

Without saying anymore words, he lifted the bottom of my sundress until he got it over my ass. Usually, the dresses were supposed to fit a little looser than the average dresses. On me, this dress snugged against my body. I felt the ripples as they waved through my fat ass. I wasn't afraid, nor ashamed to say it. My ass was big, soft, and round. I took pride in that shit.

"Damn, girl." Rell dug his fingertips into my booty, giving me a lovely feeling massage. He was massaging my booty so good, my pussy was getting wet. I could feel the cream between my legs dripping down my thighs. Oh shit. I was cumming and he hadn't really done anything.

Gotdamn, what was this man doing to me? Lawd, Jesus, Mary, and Joseph, one of y'all help a bitch out!

I was so into the booty rub, I hadn't felt him probe for my pussy lips until his index and middle finger were inside. Instantly, I began to rock against his fingers. "Rel-lll…I want…"

I couldn't even get my words out. He was working my pussy so good, I was standing in a squatting position and riding them shits.

"You want what, baby? What you want from daddy?" His deep, husky voice caressed my eardrum. He also licked, then sucked my earlobe. Fuck this, I couldn't take it anymore!

"I want you to fuck me, daddy," I whispered, out of breath. He was going in a slow and steady pace at first. He was now picking the pace up.

"Say it louder, Rizz. Say that shit like you mean that shit!" he barked, pressing me against the door. He even managed to get one of my meaty thighs up and over his broad ass shoulder. The other was struggling to hold the rest of my weight. If he wasn't pressing so hard, I'd fall my ass on this floor.

"I want you to fuck mee!" I sang it louder. The heat mixed with juices flowing from my southern tunnel was overlapping his fingers. If they were people, they'd be goners. That's how wet Rell had me right now.

Soon, he replaced his fingers with his dick. I scooted back some because his girth being slammed into me was a bit much. "Nah, bring yo ass here, girl."

If this ol' DC Young Fly ass nigga… "Shiiit, slow d-d-down, baby. It's too much!" I screamed.

Rell only picked up the pace, and my other leg as well. He was now squeezing the life out my ass while attempting to fracture my pelvis. This nigga was balls deep. It hurt so bad, it felt damn good. I hadn't had dick like this in...shit, never. No man had ever beat my shit up like Rell. Even the first time we fucked, he showed me who was boss.

If that didn't scare me the most, I don't know what. I liked to be in control of everything. With Israel's spoiled ass, that was impossible. He stood back and let me do me sometimes. Other than that, he was shutting my ass up and kicking me out his car for spitting sly shit.

I was pissed for weeks. His uglass had the audacity to kick me out his stank ass car. He asked me about Sean, I gave a simple answer. Rell wanted me to drop my nigga and get with him. He was demanding like that. All the Casique men were, actually. I wasn't about to give him the satisfaction.

Besides, Rell was too mentally unstable to be dealing with another situation. Especially one with my ass. I needed his undivided attention. His mind was too occupied on killing his baby mother—another reason I wasn't fucking with him like that. He had a whole pregnant hoe. Then, trying to get me trapped. I was on IUD. This shit has been effective for too long for me to be getting pregnant now.

"Nah, take this shit baby." He literally peeled me off the door. My back was so sticky from sweat. I may as well have been glued to it. So sticky, if he moved me too fast, my skin might be left on the door.

"Shiiiit!" He held one of my legs over his shoulders and wrapped the other one around his waist. This nigga had me doing different shit I didn't know my big ass could do.

"Yeah, take this shit, baby. Take daddy's dick…" He slid his tongue in my mouth, sucking my tongue and slamming his dick into me deeper. This time, he was being gentle, yet deep. He was taking me to new levels. That's all I knew and needed to know.

"Rellll!" I shrieked.

"Take this shit off!" he demanded. He was referring to my sundress and shoes. He was sending out demands yet fucking the shit out of me. I looked at him like, *nigga!* "Fuck it. I'll do it."

He then snatched my sandals off, throwing them both in different directions. Then, he snatched my sundress off. When I heard the shit rip, I almost hopped off his dick. He must've felt my ass jerk, about to move. He grabbed a handful of my ass and squeezed it.

"Fuck that dress. I'll buy you another one sometime this week." He spoke in a promising tone.

He was biting my neck and sucking it, walking toward the bathroom in the room. "Rell, please don't give me no fucking hickies!"

Smack!

"I can do whatever I want to my wife." He slapped my ass.

"Nigga, I ain't ya wife."

"My fiancée then," he corrected himself.

"Israel, I ain't that either." I rolled my eyes, speaking in a dry tone. He was carrying us in the shower. Turning the water on, it sprouted from every corner of the shower walls. "My hair! Oh my gawd! It's getting wet!"

"Shut up and come wash ya husband up." He put me

down on wobbly legs. I had to hold onto him to regain my balance at first.

"You ain't my husband, nigga." I sneered at him. He was taking this shit way too far. That's one of the things I hated about Rell. He did the absolute most. I couldn't help but to love his uglass, though.

"I am your husband, and you are my wife. We're engaged, Rizz. Whether you want to believe it or not, I don't give a fuck. This shit you got going on with that square ass nigga you thought was cool to bring up in here is over as of now. Let me catch you with that nigga and I swear, I'm bodying homeboy."

"Any other nigga who you think you're about to bring into the picture next, too. Test my truth if you want to, baby girl. You know my gun still bangs, in and out the game, ma. Now, wash your husband up so I can finish fucking you!"

Damn. He didn't have to shoot me twice. I followed his request before he had my ass pinned in another position. This nigga was crazy, but he was right. I didn't want to test his gangster.

As far as Sean, I'd have to figure out what to do with him later. It kind of hurt my feelings. I was just getting to know him and catching these heavy feelings for him. At this point, I wanted to have my cake and eat it too. My *husband* would kill my ass too, though.

☙❧

After Rell had me bent over, touching my toes while he dug me out from the back, we were lying in bed in each other's arms. Just like the times before, it felt good—right. I wasn't out of touch with reality, though.

Rell might've said what he wanted about the whole husband shit. That wasn't flying, though. He'd fucked me so good. I was agreeing to just about anything—during! He could've told me the sun was out and blue at night. I would've believed him because of the sexual feelings he was taking me through. Now that the sexual high was coming down, I had to address him about his recent testament.

"Rell?" I called out to him.

"Yeah, baby?" he groggily answered.

"I meant what I said about us…" I was circling my finger around his pecks.

"Rizz…" He blew out a breath. I knew he was becoming frustrated. I didn't care, though. He could get as mad as he wanted.

"I'm being serious, Rell. We are not together. I'm with Sean and I mean it, okay?" I made myself clear.

I loved Rell, and Lord knew I wanted to be with him. I wasn't doing it like this, though. Not with all this mess going on. I was his best friend, no matter what. Us being together would have to wait, though.

"Rell, I know you heard me." I shook him. This nigga was pretending to snore now. "Israel, I swear…" I raised my hand to slap his ass. I bet he'd wake his ass up then.

He grabbed me by the wrist before my palm could connect with his face. "Yo, you slap me, and I promise, I'll be the last nigga you ever lay eyes on again, Rizz. I heard ya bucket head ass the first time. You can say or do what you want, for real. Just know I keep my promises."

He then turned over, putting his back to mine. I can't

lie, I didn't like the shit. Him turning his back to me left me cold. Nothing was colder than his words, though. I knew for a fact that there was truth in them.

He also knew for a fact that I didn't take threats well, and I loved a challenge. I wasn't Keyona. Rell didn't have to ask about me because he knew. That little smack to his head moved his sense around. He needed to chill for real.

CHAPTER 6

KORI

As I laid in the bed in the room I picked, I shivered some. With it being summer, I thought it'd be warmer. I guess it was true what they said about global warming. Either that or summer was skipping us on the east coast.

Snuggling the blankets over my shoulder and under my chin, I was curled in the fetal position. This was the best way to keep myself warm.

I stared at the clock as it read close to one o'clock in the morning. My mind drifted off to my mama. I'd gone out to Portland and flew back to Chicago with her.

I planned on spending my Fourth of July with her. We were going to cook, stay up watching movies, and watch the fireworks pop off from my backyard. I had a nice view of the show they put on downtown every year.

I just knew she'd enjoy herself. I was also praying that this trip brought back some good memories and she'd want to move back home. After all, this was her home, born and raised. I grew up listening to her compare her 'stomping grounds' to the ones in Portland. I didn't get it. Why not just move back?

Creeek

I jumped up in the bed when I heard the door open. Quickly, I reached over and clicked the light on. Lah was standing there, eyeballing me, looking stupid. I rolled my eyes at him and crossed my arms over my chest. This nigga had some nerve to come into my room.

We hadn't spoken in almost a week. He didn't try to call or come by. What made him think I wanted to see him now?

Rolling my eyes, I sucked in a deep breath. "What do you want, Islah?"

"You." He shrugged, walking into the room like I wasn't pissed at him. He got in the bed and slid under the covers with me. He was trying to wrap his arms around me, pulling me closer.

As bad as I wanted to give in, I gave him the cold shoulder. "You have a funny ass way of showing it."

I wanted to love all over him. I wanted to hump his fine ass. Even in just pajama bottoms and a simple wife beater, my man was everything. His lips and beard got me every time. I loved the way it felt tickling against my neck when he was trying to get some. That was another thing.

We hadn't had sex in two weeks. It was my idea to stop. Of course, he wasn't with the idea. I didn't care. I wanted to give us some time to get to know one another without the sex.

"What you mean?" he asked dumbfoundedly.

"I mean, you ain't called or text me all week—like, at

all. So, how you say you miss me?" I spat, staring him upside the head.

"First, I never said I missed you. I said *want* you. Second, you a damn lie. I came by you weren't there. I also called you, you didn't answer the phone."

"You called me *one* time, Islah. I was out of town getting my mother when you came by. But you'd know that if you kept calling!" I raised my voice at him.

"You a grown ass woman. If you wanted to hear from me, you got my number. Another thing, baby girl I'm not going to tell again about how you talk to me." He cleared his throat. "How do you know I didn't feel like talking on the phone? Maybe *I was going through something* and couldn't get to the phone. Huh? Why you ain't call and check up on your nigga, since you so pressed? Oh, right, *it's all about Kori*, right?"

He called himself trying to check me. I wasn't about to let him flip this shit on me though. "Tuh, nigga please. I don't feel bad about being mad. You can't make me feel bad. If there was something going on, you're supposed to *call and tell me*. How else am I supposed to know?!"

"You're supposed to call! Check on your nigga if your nigga ain't checked on you. That's street code 101, baby girl. Same shit applies here. Now, are you gon' let me hold you, or are you about to bitch all night?" he clapped his hands as he spoke.

Slightly, I turned my head, throwing daggers in the side of his head. This nigga didn't even consider how I felt! He was making it all about him.

"As a matter of fact, no. Get out my room, Islah. I'm sick of you," I demanded.

He sat his ass there, staring me upside the head. We were in a full-blown stare down now. I was fighting like crazy not to look away. I was pissed and wanted to show him just how much. Or else my ass would be sand between his fingers.

"Oh, that's how you feel?" he asked. I didn't answer. I shrugged with one eyebrow up. "Aight. Cool then."

Once he left the room, I hit the light. Before going to bed, I turned on my favorite Pandora station; *Soul Trap*.

H.E.R x "Losing" filled the room from my phone speakers. I listened to the words, meditated on them for a few minutes.

"I'll start losing patience when my effort's being wasted…" I sang along, feeling that part the most.

I could understand that Lah has never been in a real relationship. He also wasn't showing that he wanted to be in one with me. It didn't take rocket science to know to call your girl and check up on her.

In the moment, I didn't feel like I was wrong. It was up to him to fix this, not me.

৩✖৩

The next morning, I joined the family for a late breakfast. Lah wasn't at the table, surprisingly. I wasn't exactly mad about it either. Then again, I wasn't thrilled. A part of me wanted to inquire his whereabouts. The thought left just as quickly as it came.

Being with Islah Casique was bittersweet. Bitter because he was rude as hell. He didn't know how to show proper emotion. With all the years I took psychology, I couldn't read his ass for nothing. That was the thing; he was different.

While it irked my soul, it intrigued me. It made me want to know more about him. That's what made being around him sweet. He took me out of my comfort zone. I used to be afraid of doing certain things.

He had me looking and feeling differently about life. Like, it was so much more worth doing. So much more worth living for. Low-key, these vast feelings were scary. They were also intriguing.

I was R-Kelly as fuck in this situation. My mind was telling me no, but my body was saying hell yes. That's another reason I wanted to slow down and cut sex out our relationship for a while. I wanted to focus on him as a person and get to know him for him. Not what he could do to my body with his.

"Good morning, my baby Kori." Ms. Kayla kissed me on the forehead. It threw me off because it was unexpected. I had so much respect for Ms. Kayla.

I'd heard so much about her through Rizz, and a little from Lah. The woman was a straight beast. It kind of scared me when I met her. I didn't know what to expect. I assumed she'd be mean. She was the furthest thing, though.

"Good morning, Ms. Kayla." Cheerfully, I greeted her with a warm smile. Kayla was so beautiful. I'd learned that she was mixed with Black and Indian.

She had smooth Nutella-colored skin, making her look exotic. Her eyes were black and slanted. When she smiled, they almost closed. That reason alone had me assuming she was mixed with Chinese at first. I was wrong. Lah laughed in my face one night after I asked him his mother's nationality. Asshole.

Aside from her beautiful features, her body was banging. Kayla had a tight body. You wouldn't think she pushed four kids out her cooch. Now, supposedly, she wanted a fifth. I didn't know how old she was. Nor did I ask her.

"Oh no, baby. Everyone in this family calls me Mom or Ma. Well, expect Perez. He calls me…*anyway*. None of that *Ms. Kayla* shit." I admired how she kept it real.

"Yes, Ms—Ma," I quickly corrected myself. She squinted her eyes at me, then smiled. I felt the love radiating off her to me.

"What y'all trying to get into tonight? I'm trying to do something out the box before we go camping tomorrow." Liz asked, rubbing her hands together like she was up to no good. Which she probably was.

"Whatever you're thinking, I'm down," Yanna chimed in. At first, Isi was looking down at a newspaper, then he looked up.

"If she down, I'm going too," he stated with finality.

"Nah, bro. This is a girl's only trip. Sorry." Liz Kanye-shrugged her brother.

"Shit, I guess I'm wearing a wig today then, huh. I know one of y'all brought one of them lace fronts. Rizz?" He looked to her, sitting across the table from Rell. She flipped him the bird, chewing on her food.

"Kori? You got one? Never mind, don't answer that. You the only natural one here. Either way, y'all not going alone. We in another nigga's town. Then, we out in the woods. Nah, not having it." Isi continued to shake his head at the idea.

Liz was cackling like Elmo. "That nigga just said he's wearing a wig?"

"Damn straight," Isi answered. I shook my head, laughing. I swear, there was never a dull moment in this family. I was happy to be a part of it. By blood or loyalty, it didn't make one difference to me.

"Isi, let they asses go if they want. Let em' get their asses ate up by an alligator man or some shit," Rell spat before slurping the milk and cereal he was eating out a bowl.

I turned slightly in my seat to see his face. He was glaring at Rizz something serious. Now, I was really, ready for this girl's night out. Rizz had some explaining to do. I was going to pick her brain.

Other than that, her new boyfriend wasn't here. What was up with that? She'd been raving about bringing him on this trip. Where was he at? I had a feeling it had something to do with the way Rell was glaring at her.

"Man—" Isi was going to say something to his ignorant brother, but Ma shut him down first.

"We're going out without the men, Isiah. Yanna, you got me if I got you?" She looked to her daughter-in-law.

"You already know." Yanna slapped five with her.

"Rizz? Kori? Liz?" She pointed to us as she said our names.

"You already know!" me and Rizz spoke at the same time.

"Is that even a question, Ma? You know how I get down." Liz nodded to her mother. Kayla smirked at her daughter.

"Issa done deal then."

"Issa?" Rell and Isi asked with scrunched up faces.

"What we tell you about slang, Ma?" Liz laughed out loud.

"Yeah, issa nigga," Ma checked them both. "Ohhh, Issa (eesa). Yanna, Isi! Y'all should name my future grandbaby Issa Kay (Eesa Kay)."

"Ooh! I like that. Baby, I like that!" Yanna jumped up and down, patting Isi. He smiled wholeheartedly at his wife, then they shared a kiss. One word…GOALS!

"Sounds good to me, baby." he said before kissing her again.

"Oh, and Kori?" Kayla put her finger up. She was chewing her food and staring at me. After swallowing, she said, "You and Islah's baby gon' be named Karah or Koran. That's spelled with a K."

I spit my juice back into the cup before I had the chance to swallow it. "I beg your pardon?"

"Yup." She nodded. "Rizz, you and Rell's babies gon' be named Parell and Parizz. It's going to be a boy and a girl," Ma confidently stated. What was it with old people and being so confident about the future?

"Look, Ma. You know I love you, but I don't think so." Rizz shook her head with her nose up.

"I believe it, Ma. Keep on talking the future up. We're getting married too, huh?" Rell chimed in with his two cents. Rizz daggered the evil eyes at him.

"Now, I ain't say all of that boy. Y'all having twins, though." Ms. Kayla said with much clarity.

"What makes you think this?" I asked.

The next person coming into the room was Mama Casique. She was smoking that cigarette that smelled like weed again. She was also wearing the same bathrobe, but with matching tube socks. Her short, light brown hair was scattered on top of her head. It reminded me of the Trickster's hair from *The Flash*.

"Rizz is already pregnant with the twins." she said, pulling on the cigarette and blowing out the smoke. Standing away from the kitchen table, she leaned against the marble countertop.

"No offense, Mama, but like *hell* I am! Don't be jinxing me." Paris spat with irritation. Rell slammed his bowl down on the counter, then he proceeded to walk out the room.

Paris mumbled something smart under her breath, but I heard her loud and clear. "Big ass kid."

I agreed with her. His attitude about these lies were ridiculous. I mean, no offense to his mom and grand mom. I just didn't believe what they were saying. Right now, at least.

"Paris, I'm only telling the truth. I had this dream a couple weeks back. You were giving birth to two beautiful babies. One boy and one girl." Mama Casique stated with a simple shrug.

Paris smacked her lips, arguing back. "Okay, and that doesn't mean I'm pregnant by Rell. It could be Sean's…"

The room grew silent after she said that. Thank God, Jesus, Mary, and Joseph that Rell wasn't in the room. The way he was acting, he'd have a BF (Bitch Fit).

Either way, if she was pregnant or not, the baby wasn't Sean's. Paris already confirmed she hadn't given him any. She claimed something about him was *off*.

Me, I thought she was just too caught up on her best friend. Paris could say and act how she wanted. The fact remained that she felt some type of way about Israel Casique.

"Okay Mama, enough of talking about the future. That cigaweed is working on your molecules." Kayla kindly told her mother-in-law. I didn't get how old people could sense when someone was pregnant. It was super weird to me.

The next voice we heard was Perez's. He yelled from wherever he was in the house. "I smell cigaweed!" Mama Casique put her cigaweed out and slipped it into her robe pocket right before he entered the room. "Mama…"

"Perez…" She smiled. "Good morning, mijo."

"Mama, you been smoking again?" he asked with a questioning stare. She pursed her lips together and shook her head no.

"Of course not, mijo. Where would I get it from? You stole my stash, remember? I hope you're not smoking it. *It plays with your molecules.*" She played along with her lie. Perez was about to say something until the kitchen door leading to outside opened.

In walked Lah with his Beats blasting. They were so loud, we could hear Beyoncé x Sorry.

I peeped how sweaty he was. His entire face and wife beater were drenched. I couldn't help but be turned on by him. That, and plus we hadn't had sex since the last time we were together. I just wanted to lick the sweat off his face and chest.

Maybe I need some D, I told myself.

No, no, no, Kori. You need to make him wait until he thinks about how he made you feel, I told myself.

"What's up, family?" he spoke to everyone. The fact that he never looked my way had me in my feelings. It was like he was trying to pretend I wasn't in the room. This nigga was as rude as they came.

After he left the room, an idea popped into my head. "Let's go out and have some drinks tonight. Well, not Paris. Since she *pregnant* and all." I winked at her. She flipped me the bird.

"You a damn lie." She rolled her eyes as well.

"Yaass! We can hit the club up after we go to the Escape Room," Liz added with excitement.

"Bish, who going to the escape room?" Yanna asked like she wasn't down for it. I'd never been, but I was for it. Something new and different might be just what I needed this weekend.

"Bish," Liz mimicked Yanna. "You and the rest of the family. I think it'll be fun. These rooms help build relationships, we work together, and it's fun."

Yanna looked like she was still iffy. "I don't know. I always thought of those rooms as some paranormal activity shit going on. Like people go missing."

I couldn't help but to laugh. Liz, Ma, Mama, and Paris joined in. Even Isi was laughing at her comment. The only one who hadn't spoken on it was Perez. He'd been on his phone since trying to scold Mama. For this to be 'family' time, he had a lot going on.

Lah had told me that his dad was a workaholic. Also, Perez was grooming Isi to take over their businesses. Perez wanted to sit back so he could enjoy his family like he always dreamed. I didn't blame him. He was fifty. It was time for him to sit back and see the fruits of his labor in prosperity.

"No, it's nothing like that. It'll be fun, sis!" Liz stood up from the table, jumping up and down. I giggled a little. Liz was always fun and funny to be around. She kept the vibe mellowed. She was someone you wanted to keep around you.

After Yanna agreed, Liz was even more excited. She did a headcount and managed to get us in at the last minute. I was just as excited as she was. Lah entered my mind and left just as fast. If he wanted to act like I didn't exist this weekend, I'd do the same. Two can play this game.

CHAPTER 7

LAH

That escape room shit was hard! I went in with a clear mindset, thinking the shit would be a piece of cake. Wrong. That shit chewed me up and spit me back out. I had a whole fucking headache from dealing with those riddles.

Then, I also had Kori on the brain. I was trying hard to rid her ass out of my mind. It wasn't working though. She wanted me to apologize for not hitting her up. The way I saw it, if she was so pressed, she could've hit me up. I mean, come on. We in the twentieth century. Grow the fuck up, Kori! I guess she was used to niggas kissing her ass.

"Welcome to *Ripples*. Can I get you something to drink?" the bottle girl came up to me and asked. I checked her out from where she was standing. Shorty was cute. She wore hip-hugging jeans that looked especially made for her. I mean, they were painted on baby girl, and only she knew how to remove them without a wrinkle. My eyes moved up her body. She was also wearing a baby tee. It cut off right above her belly button. She had a diamond belly ring too and she was cute in the face. With light brown skin, slanted dark brown eyes, small pouty lips, and a cute little button nose, she was average, but cute. Shorty was flirting with me too.

"Yeah, get me a Henny off the rocks." I threw her a sly side smirk. She smiled, giggled, and put the empty tray she was carrying under her arm. She was stopped before walking away.

"Um, excuse you!" Rizz called out to her. The bottle girl stopped in her tracks and turned around. She had a questioning expression on her face. "While you *a-he-he-ha-in in this nigga face*, you forgot to ask the rest of us what we wanted!"

I cracked up because baby girl's face turned beet red. Sis ain't have to do her like that. "Damn, Rizz. Let her live."

"Um, boo!" She threw her hand up in my face and turned her attention back to the girl. "*Well?*"

"Oh, um, what would y'all like?" the bottle girl nervously asked. After everybody put their order in, she walked away with her tail between her legs. I bet she was gon' cry in the breakroom. Baby girl came over with all the confidence. All it took was for Rizz to snatch that ass and her shine was gone. Now, she was unattractive to me in the worst way. Any bitch that let another take their happiness was weak to me. She wasn't real and couldn't ride in my car.

"Why you do baby like that, Rizzy?" Ma asked, cracking the hell up. She wasn't even quiet about it. Rizz smacked her teeth.

"Because Ma, she was allll up in over here. This nigga

has a whole female. She was skinning and grinning in my bro face and didn't even acknowledge us. That was disrespectful!"

"I hear you, baby girl." Ma agreed.

"Mkaayy!" Yanna slapped hands with her.

Next, Rizz turned to Kori. "And what the fuck? You a mute now? The bitch was in your man's face. You should've said something. It wasn't my place, but since you're my sister, I couldn't let it slide."

Kori scrunched her face up, looking at her crazy. "Girl, I'm single. She could've spoken to bro all she wanted."

Her statement caused me to turn abruptly in my seat. I know damn well she wasn't showing her ass. Oh, this nigga was big mad. She lucky Pops and Ma was sitting amongst us. I'd snatch her little ass up. She was one blessed woman right now. She knew the shit too.

"Oh hell, see...y'all too much for me." Rizz shook her head. She had her nerve saying anything when she had Rell sitting in his feelings. "Oh, yes! Drinks!"

The bottle girl, whose name was Kas, set the drinks on the table. Speaking of *that delirious one*, she'd been blowing me up for the past few days. She was blowing my shit up with text messages and phone calls. I was sending that bitch to voicemail each time.

"Didn't Mama tell you not to be drinking?" Yanna asked Rizz as she threw her shots back.

"I know, but I ain't preg—"

"But nothing, Rizz! Put the liquor down." Rell barked.

I was too busy glaring at 'sis' ass to worry about what they were beefing about. Kori had me fucked up if she thought I was going to sit and let her play me like a bitch nigga. I already told her she was gon' learn about me.

"Ooouuu! This is my soong!" Rizz hopped out her seat and started twerking her backside like an energetic snake. Still, I was glaring at her cousin.

Kori saw me see her from her. I don't know why she even trying to play me right now. She kept wiping the side of her face and neck like it was sweaty or some shit. She just felt my eyes burning on her skin and couldn't take the pressure. Kori knew she'd fucked up. It was cool. I had something for that ass. All she needed was some dick.

"Fuck it up, Rizz!" Yanna and Kori cheered her drunk ass on.

I shook my head as I slow sipped my Henny. This was turning out to be a reenactment of Pops' birthday. Only we didn't have Keyona's bitch ass around, which made it better. I loved when the fam was all together, and we were all getting along good. Besides Mama, everybody that mattered to me was right here in this room.

"Oohhh! This. Is. My. Song! Don't even play with me right now!" Kori got up and started twerking with Rizz.

Even though we were way up in VIP, there were a bunch of niggas around. They were all watching her shake her ass in that little ass glitter dress she called herself twerking in. Who taught her how to bounce her ass? Miley Cyrus or some shit?

A nigga walking by stopped to watch. He had a whole half glass of Henny, just sipping the shit and eyeballing my bitch.

"Aye homie, move the fuck along! Ain't shit to see here." I stood up in his face. He put his hands up, slowly backing up. I knew he didn't want these problems.

"And you!" I snatched Kori's hot in the booty ass up.

"Put me down, Islah! Let me go!" She beat my back.

Yup. This was a repeat of Pops' birthday. Only it wasn't his birthday, and Kori was my girl now.

I ignored her ass all the way until we got to the ladies' room. Setting her on her feet, I pushed her inside the biggest stall. I didn't care who was in this bitch. Kori was about to get cussed out and then get this dick.

"Bro, you're tripping. Get off me!" She punched my chest as hard as she could. I stood in place, allowing her a minute to continue punching me in the chest. She packed a mean punch, but not so much they'd knock the air out of me. I can't lie, my ass might've been laid out for a hot minute if she punched hard enough.

Once she finished punching me, she was out of breath. I stood there watching her chest heave up and down. I searched her eyes for tears but didn't see any. I always took Kori as the crying type. Either she was playing it tough, or I had her wrong.

"Why are you acting like you don't have to fucking man? Shaking your ass in front of other niggas, being disrespectful to me—in my face at that!" I got closer to her, barking in her face.

She looked at me like I was the one who'd just fucked up. Without flinching and so much heart, she clarified, "I don't have a man. Who my man? You?"

"Kori…I swear you testing me right now." I had to take a step back to refrain from wrapping my hands around her fucking neck.

This was the shit I couldn't do. This was one of the reasons I hadn't taken a bitch seriously. I wasn't sure of what I'd do when they became disrespectful. My feelings for Kori, though, the shits weren't going nowhere. I had to face them and straighten shit out between us.

"My man wouldn't leave me thinking the worst and not reaching out to me. My man would know when to apologize when he's in the wrong. Not make me feel like my feelings don't matter! So, again…what man?!" She continued to scream on me.

"You still off that dumb shit from last night, man?" I kissed my gums and stepped back some. Shaking my head at her, I glared at her.

Her nostrils flared as she glared back at me. "See, this is exactly what I'm talking about! You don't care about how I feel! I can't deal, Lah…" She shook her head with a sad expression.

"You can deal with it. If I can, you can," I stated with affirmation. Any other female and I would've let her go. Not Kori, though. I wasn't going to let her go just because we had one little argument.

"Islah, I'm serious—"

"I'm sorry baby, okay?" I cut her off. I knew my ass had to apologize. That was the only way to squash this shit. I didn't like dwelling on the same shit. Kori wasn't going to let the shit go until I apologized.

"You're what?" She looked at me like she was shocked.

I blew out a deep breath. Why females always want you repeat shit? "You heard me."

"What you sorry for?" she quizzed with a smirk.

See, now she was just playing games. I wasn't going to play them with her. I grabbed her by the neck and gently pushed her against the bathroom wall. Kori was rubbing her hands all over my arms and chest.

Lifting her chin, I pressed my lips against hers. She was moaning and we weren't even doing anything yet. Leaning down closer, I reached under her dress, attempting to snatch her panties off. When I felt only her bare pussy, I got mad as fuck and slammed her hard as fuck against the stall.

"The fuck you ain't got no panties on for?!" I barked and glared at her ass. She looked frightened. Like I was about to beat her ass or something. "Answer me!"

"I-I-I…" she stuttered. "I thought—"

"You thought what?!" I couldn't keep my voice down for nothing. The fuck she rolling around a different city with no panties on for? Any city, for that matter! Then, she had on this little tight ass dress. She had me fucked up!

"I did it to make you mad, okay?" she confessed in a whiny tone. She also had a little slur going on. She'd consumed a few drinks with Rizz and Yanna's drunk asses.

"Wooow, yo! Well, guess what, ma? You've accomplished your goal because I'm heated!" I slapped my hand against the bathroom wall, closest to her head. She flinched and moved a little.

"Lah, I'm so—"

"I don't want to hear shit, Kori. Bring yo ass on. We're going home, now!" I snatched her by the hand and pulled her out the bathroom.

We made it back to our table. Rell had Rizz thrown over his shoulder. She was slurring some obscenities at him. It all fell on deaf ears. I noticed the car keys in his hands. At first, I shrugged it off. Then, I remembered we all rolled in a van together.

"Nope. Y'all asses better take a damn Uber, Lyft, cab or something." I snatched the keys out his hands. This was looking like a repeat of Pops' birthday alright, only this time, Rell and Rizz's asses weren't leaving us in this club.

"Come on Lah, Rizz need to get home and lay down. I ain't gon' leave y'all this time. Ma, Pops, and them coming too." Rell explained with pleading eyes. He wasn't lying. Ma walked up behind me.

"Y'all okay?" She placed her hand on my back and Kori's arms. Kori looked to me to answer Ma. "Well?"

"Nah, but we will be." I assured her with a kiss on the cheek. I didn't need her stressing over me and Kori's shit. Ma had her own problems with Pops.

I knew something wasn't right between them. My room was next door to theirs. The main reason I went to Kori's room was I overheard them arguing. Ma kept asking Pops about the guy that favored Isi. Pops kept replying with little shit like, 'leave it alone' or 'let's talk about this when we get back to Chicago'.

I had gone to the kitchen to run some water and get my thoughts together. That didn't seem to be working. I was on Kori's bad side. I had ignored my girl for a whole week. I knew I wasn't going to get in her room easily. Yet, I needed to be under her to gain some peace for the night.

I wasn't used to being up a chick's ass 25/8. Being single for so long, I loved my space. I loved that I could come and go. I wasn't trying to treat Kori like a jump-off either. I just…just didn't think to reach out. This shit was still all too new for me. I had to do better to keep her happy.

Knock, knock,

"Come in," I answered the person on the other side of

the door, from my bed. I'd been lying here thinking about everything. This night could've gone so much better.

Creeek...

Looking toward the door, I spotted Kori's creeping ass standing there. She stood there in the doorway, dressed in boy shorts and a tank. On her face was a solemn expression.

"What you want?" I asked the same question she asked last night. As I said, I didn't hold grudges. I was pissed, yes, yet I'd hear her out.

"You," she answered with the same response I had to hers.

Patting the empty spot next to me, I summoned her. "Come on."

She came over and got under the blankets with me.

"Are you still mad at me?" she asked, hanging her head in low solemn.

"I was never *mad* at you. I was disappointed for the most part."

I watched her head shoot up like one of those whack-a-mole games. "Disappointed?"

"Yup." I gave a simple shrug with a simple answer.

I was heated with her at the club. So heated, I wanted to choke the life out of her. Upset with me or not, see should've known better. We ain't been together a month, but she still knows how I get down.

Out in public with no panties on? Only a lame nigga would've thought that shit was okay. He probably would've become turned on and fucked her right there in the ladies' room. I found it disrespectful in the worst way. She probably wasn't expecting my reaction. Like shit would be copacetic after the apology and me finding her with no fucking underwear on.

"Islah—" she started to say.

"Do you know why I like you so much, Kori?"

She was silent as she stared me in the eyes. I raised my eyebrows at her, waiting for her response. She shrugged her shoulders, shaking her head. "I don't know. Why?"

"You're different from other bit—*females* I usually entertain. You don't do basic bitch shit. You're a breath of fresh air for me. You make me want to get to know you. I think I told you before. I don't know shit about relationships. With you, I want to learn."

I was only speaking from my heart. Moments like this, I always thought of as for soft niggas. I was learning, though. There's absolutely nothing wrong with expressing your feelings. Being with Kori has taught me that. She was always having these 'heart to hearts', getting to know me and trying to pick my brain.

"Again, I'm sorry Lah—"

"Who?"

"Islah," she muttered under her breath. "I'm sorry. It was stupid and immature of me. I was just mad and thought it'd get your attention. I see that it did, but not in a good way."

"That was some childish ass shit, ma. I don't care how mad you are with me. Don't do no more hoe shit like that again, Kori."

She nodded, placing her head back down. I knew she felt ashamed. That wasn't in her character at all. While I was telling her how I felt, I had to tell her how she made me feel as well.

"Hey." Placing my index finger under her chin, I

lifted her face so that her beautiful brown eyes could look back in mine. "I like you the way you are. You don't have to go all out like that to get my attention. Just be yourself. I also apologize for making you feel like you had to do something like that. It started with me. I was in the wrong for not being a better boyfriend. You forgive me?"

She nodded her head. I watched her eyes to see if there would be any waterworks. I don't know why, but for the life of me, I wanted to see her cry. Not like on no negative type shit. It was just something about when a female cried at the right moment.

"Come here." I pulled her onto my lap. I didn't even have to tell her to give me a kiss. She just knew I wanted her lips on mine. Kissing her was life being breathed into me. This time was no different.

"I missed you, real shit." I confessed.

"I missed you more." Her voice cracked as she threw her arms around my neck.

"Show me how much." I seductively whispered in her ear.

She pulled away, popping me on the shoulder. "Nuh uhn, Islah. You ain't slick."

"What? We still getting to know each other?"

"It's not just about getting to know one another. It's about us building a connection and learning to lo—*like* each other without sex. Like, what if sex wasn't involved? Could you really see us together?"

I didn't miss her almost saying love. Love. That was a whole other conversation. We were still in the like phase. At least I was, anyway. I couldn't tell if Kori was yet. I knew we'd eventually get there.

"You're right...I can't be with you without sex involved."

"Lah!"

I cracked a smile. "I'm just playing, baby. But, can I get head on the weekends?"

"Lah!" She popped me again.

"I'm just playing. Every Wednesday?" I joked. She raised her hand to pop me again. This time, I dodged it and grabbed her hands.

"You so irky," she giggled. "Besides, even if that were a thing, I don't give head."

I was shocked by her confession. This was a first. I thought females loved giving head. "Really? Why not?"

"I promised myself I'd reserve that for my husband. I feel like oral sex should only be with one person. The one you're going to spend the rest of your life with."

Damn. Was this girl reading my diary or what? "Wow. That's crazy."

"Really? Why?"

"I feel the same way. I never gave a chick head before. Just like you, I promised it was going to be for the one I wanted to spend the rest of my life with."

A smile broke her hard expression. "Well, let's start planning the wedding!"

She was laughing hysterically, but I knew she was serious. "Let's finish getting to know each other first."

"That part!" she screamed, laughing. I joined her in laughter. I loved the sound of her voice, laughing and happy. This was what I missed the most. I might've said I wanted sex, but it wasn't just that. It was more than just a physical attraction with us.

Crash!

"What was that?" Kori jumped out my lap like the noise was coming from inside our room.

I reached in the drawer inside the night table, grabbing my gun. "I don't know. Stay here while I go check shit out."

"No, I'm going with you." She began pacing around the room like a nervous wreck.

"Baby, stay your ass here. You don't know what's out there." I laughed at her. She was talking about going but looked scared as hell.

"I know, but you're going out there."

"I'll be back. Stay. Here." I pointed at her, speaking in a stern voice before rushing out the room.

Entering the hallway, I bumped into Isi and Rell. Both of them had their guns. Isi nodded his head in one direction to me, and in another to Rell. That meant for us to cover him on either side.

Crash!

We heard the noise again. It was like something had broken. The closer we got to where the noise was coming from, it got louder. There were also voices.

Crash!

"Kayla, I'm not doing this shit with you tonight. I fucked up, okay?! Can you let the shit go now?"

"Oh no, baby. You're doing this. I asked you, Perez! I asked you did you end things with that bitch? You said you did! Now, over twenty years later, she has a son that looks exactly like mine?!"

"Kayla—"

"Fuck you, Perez!"

Crash!

"Throw another fucking glass at me and see that I don't

snatch your ass!" Pops' voice rose an octave.

I didn't know what exactly they were arguing about tonight. This was a rerun of last night. This was the reason I couldn't sleep and needed to be under Kori.

When Pops raised his voice, he meant business. It'd been a while since I heard him yell at Ma. I always hated it. Since I was a kid, seeing or even hearing my parents argue put knots in my stomach.

"Man, I'm tired of this shit. All they do is fight these days. We have to do something about this dude that looks just like Isi." I breathed out in frustration. Isi and Rell looked to me.

"We're going to find him. As for Ma and Pops, this is between them. It's hard to listen to, I know because I hate the shit too. They gon' be alright, though," Isi assured, like only a big brother could.

"He's right. Let's go back to bed," Rell backed him. I nodded, turning on my heels to go back to my room.

"Ahhh, Perez baby…I…"

"You what, baby? Shit…"

Tell me I wasn't hearing my parents having sex.

"Are they?" Rell asked, referring to our parents.

"Yep." Isi nodded with a perplexed look on his face.

Well, I'm officially scarred for life.

When I got back to the room, Kori was cuddled up under the covers in the bed. I climbed in behind her and wrapped her up in my arms. After turning off the night lamp, I kissed her on the forehead.

"Turn on the music…" she told me sleepily.

Scary ass.

CHAPTER 8

RELL

Once again, I was nursing Rizz back to health. I was lying in bed beside her, rubbing her back as she peacefully slept. I listened to her lightly snoring. I wanted it to be like this every night.

Like Ol' girl Tynisha Kelli said, *'I really didn't know back then, but right now I'm totally sure'*. I wanted Rizz to be my girl, my wife, my everything. She was already my best friend with benefits. I wanted more, though. I wanted her to want it too.

I knew sooner or later I was going to push her away with my obsessive antics. I needed to chill, for real. This I knew. My head was all wrapped up and gone from this Keyona bullshit.

"Relly?" Rizz moaned out my name. I continued to rub her back.

"What's up, baby girl?" I was talking quietly because I knew she'd wake up with a hangover.

Here it was, six in the morning, and I got no sleep. I was up thinking about shit. I was also up watching Rizz sleep. I wanted to be on standby in case she had to puke or something. I didn't mind because this was my best friend.

"Where am I?" she groaned.

"You in your bed, at the lake house, ma," I answered her. Shaking my head, I geared up to answer twenty-one questions. She did this every time. It never failed.

"Relly, I have a horrible headache. How much did you let me drink last night?" she whined, laying her head against my chest. I enjoyed this moment. I didn't know how much more I'd get with her like this. She was acting so needy, and I loved it. This could be us all the time, but she was playing.

"I didn't let you drink that much. You did it on your own." I chuckled at her ass trying to blame me. She giggled, then hiccupped.

"Whatever punk, you supposed to be like—" Her sentence was cut off when she began to dry heave. Jumping out of bed, Rizz ran to the adjoining bathroom. I was right on her heels, on my knees, ready to hold her weave as she puked her guts out.

Once she was officially done, she fell against me. I already had the warm towel ready to wipe her down. Getting her to her feet, I cut the shower on. I made sure it was the right temperature before stripping her down and getting her in.

I washed her down twice thoroughly before getting her out. After drying her off, I lotioned her down and put her in a pair of my boxers and a wife beater. The entire time, she was silent as I catered to her. Before lying her back in the bed, I wrapped her hair in one of those hair tie thingies.

"R-R-Rell-ll...can you lay with m-me-e? It's s-s-oo c-cold!" Her teeth chattered and she shivered under the blankets. I was cleaning everything up.

"Yeah, Rizzy. Give me a minute..." I was in the middle of disinfecting the bathroom with Lysol wipes. The way the lemon scent had it smelling, you wouldn't know Rizz had redecorated the spot.

Once I was done, just as I promised, I went to lay with her. She pushed herself under me, her booty resting perfectly against my wood. The electrical shock waves from the chemistry between us was making me hard. Rizz must've felt me rock up. She was now grinding her ass against me.

My first instinct was to lift her leg and raw dog her ass just like she liked; roughly. Instead, I grabbed her hip, applying pressure to make her stop.

"Cut that out, ma." I demanded in a stern tone.

I wasn't going to take it there with her anymore. Not until I knew for sure she was ready for everything I had to offer. I knew I hurt her by making her feel like a second option. I was ready to show her that she was my first option, though. I wanted her to carry my last name and my kids. I wanted to wake her up in the morning with head for breakfast. I wanted to unapologetically have our corny public moments.

A lot of people would assume we were more than friends when we weren't then. Now, shit was different. I used to tell her I'd do anything for her because she was my best friend. That never would change. She'd just be my best friend, lover, and wife.

"C'mon, zaddy...you know you want it." She moaned. Fuck! She sounded so damn sexy.

She wasn't playing fair at all. She knew exactly how to

get me riled up. I almost took her up on her offer. I had to stick to my word, though. I was going to show Rizz she was more than just a best friend with benefits. She was so much more to me. She deserved everything. Right now, she was dealing with this Sean nigga. I'd let her live for now. I was coming for what was mine, though.

"Nah, Rizzy. Quit it, I'm serious." I thumped her thigh with my middle finger.

"Why are you acting like you don't want me?" she asked in a serious tone.

I turned her around so she could look me in the eyes. She laid there staring up at me, and me staring at her. I wanted her to hear me loud and clear. I wanted her to feel where I was coming from.

"I want you so fucking bad right now, ma. Like, you have no idea. But I want all of you, Rizzy. Not just a piece. Not just this." I pointed in between her legs.

"As I said before, I want you to be my wife. You have to want it too, though. I know I hurt you, Rizz. Nothing I can say will change that. I can prove it to you with my actions, though. This thing you got with Sean, I'm going to let you slide with it. Do you, ma. You deserve that. I'm always and forever going to be your best friend, though. At the end of the day, I just want you to be happy with whoever or whatever." I was speaking straight from the heart. I meant exactly what I was saying.

I watched as a small tear escaped the corner of her eye. I leaned down and kissed it away. As I was coming up, she grabbed me by the back of my neck. Pulling my lips on top of hers, she kissed me with passion. She even slid me a little tongue. Coming up for air, we were both out of breath. Like, the kiss took our breath away—literally!

"I love you so much, Israel…" she spoke, full of emotion.

"I love you more than anything, Paris." I spoke it back, my heart swelling up.

"Rell, I want to be with you, but—"

I placed my index finger against her lips. "Shhh…no buts, baby. When you ready to take that step, I'll be waiting here like *Silk* with open arms."

A huge grin spread across her face, and she let a hearty chuckle escape between her lips. "Silk? Really, nigga?"

"Hell yeah. I'm serious, girl." I laughed too. "There's a meeting in my bedroooom!"

"So, boy please don't be laa-aa-aa-te!" she sang along.

"Girl you for me, and girl me for you…" I sang.

"I don't care what people might saaay!" she added her no-singing ass two cents.

"Just ask and I'll dooo!" I cried-sang out in a hoarse tone.

"Oh my lawd. Boy, you can't sing for shit." She was laughing so hard, her face was turning red.

"You one to talk. Sounding like damn hurt horse!" I jabbed back at her, laughing.

"Whatever, punk! You love this hurt horse." She pouted.

"Hmm," I placed my thumb and index finger on my chin. "Maybe…"

"Rell!" she shrieked, swatting my arm.

"I'm just playing, boo. You know I love you." I smiled at her. She smiled back.

For the rest of the morning, we joked and reminisced until both of us fell back asleep.

CHAPTER 9
KASSIDY "KAS" KYLE

Staring at my phone, I know I didn't hear who I thought I did. I just know that wasn't my assistant, Kori, talking in the background. This low-down bitch... wait Kas, maybe it wasn't her. Maybe you just imagining this. You haven't had any sleep in three days. You're tripping, girl. Yeah, that's it.

Between Lah and Kori, I'd been blowing them both up. I was reaching out to Lah to apologize for how I acted. I was belligerent for no reason. He had every right to throw me out his home. As a result of my stupidity, I ended up in jail for a week.

That's where Kori came in. I'd called her the morning after to come and pick me up. She agreed, but never showed. So, I was forced to call the one other person I could count on.

"Girl, what's wrong with you?" my cousin, Keyona, asked me as she came prancing into the living room. She'd been crashing at my spot since she came and got me out of jail.

She only had enough in her savings to get me out. I promised I'd give her double if she used it to spring me. She also asked if she could stay with me until her and her nigga get on cool terms. I was cool with it. I mean, she was my cousin. All I asked was that she pulled her weight. She agreed and we'd been good ever since.

Since I hadn't heard from either Kori or Lah, my mind was playing tricks on me. Like, maybe they were together or something. Me thinking I heard her on the phone didn't help either.

"Girl, nothing really. I'm just trying to get ahold of my boyfriend. I haven't heard from him since I got out. Then, my shady ass assistant isn't picking up either!" I spat in an annoyed tone; the more I thought about it, the angrier I got. "I'm going to leave her a bad review. I'll end that bitch's career just before it started!"

"Girl, you didn't tell me you had a boyfriend. What's his name? Where y'all meet?" Keyona sat on the couch with me.

I rolled my eyes. I swear I told her ass I had a boyfriend. I told her when I explained how I got put in jail. I'd told her that I was acting stupid, and he put me out. I was mad and acting crazy in the elevator. I was trying to get back up to his place, but it wasn't working. The next thing I knew, I was being hauled out naked.

"His name is Lah. We met at his store. I was looking for a cute dress and he helped me." I smiled devilishly at the thought.

His charm game was up to par. He had my ass bent over in one of the dressing rooms that same day. Shit, I even sucked his dick. In return, he didn't make me pay for the dress. He said I'd paid up enough. Since then, we'd been rocking with each other. That was six months ago.

Lah had a busy schedule, so we didn't see each other a lot. I didn't trip because I knew my man was working. I never questioned his whereabouts. I didn't ask how much he cared about me. Whenever we were together, I gave it up. We smoked a blunt and sometimes, I'd cook if he was hungry. Lah was a picky eater, so he didn't always eat what was on the plate.

"Ohh! Is that right?" she asked, nodding her head. This bitch was trying to be funny. Part of the reason Keyona and I didn't hang like that is she was stuck up. Her whole family was, as a matter of fact.

"Yeah," I snidely remarked, rolling my eyes.

Keyona and I were cousins because our mothers were sisters. Her mother married rich while mine worked for everything she got. Growing up, I used to want to be like Keyona. I wanted to lavish lifestyle and money at my fingertips. Instead, I was lucky to get clothes from the thrift store. During tax season, my mom would buy me a couple of outfits and some shoes from Walmart.

I hated being poor. I hated it so much, I promised myself I'd work hard enough and never be broke again. I was going to open my own business and watch it manifest. Everything was going smoothly so far.

"So, he not answering your calls? Why?" she continued to ask about my business.

"If I knew, I'd be on the phone with him now. Don't you think?" I asked in a sarcastic tone.

"Don't shoot me cousin, dang." She put her hands up in defense. "I was only asking a question." She smirked.

I wanted to wipe the smirk off her face with my fist.

Keyona thought she was so much better than me. Suddenly, something hit me. This bitch was on my couch. Not the other way around. I should be the one asking all the questions. Not explaining shit.

"So, where is your man at? Why he kick you out?" I kindly inquired, not hiding my amusement.

"*Fiancé*, and he didn't kick me out," she corrected me in an even tone. Aww, now who was mad? I could tell she was feeling some type of way. The way her nose was flaring, and her jaw was all tightened. It was kind of funny. I could've laughed out loud right now.

"Oh? Then what exactly happened? He cheated on you or something?" I continued to torture her with my questions. She readjusted in her seat, pulling the t-shirt dress I'd lent her this morning over her knees.

"You okay?" I pressed.

She glared at me. "I'm fine. Rell didn't cheat on me. He'd never! We're just not on the same page right now. It's alright, though. We're going to get married after all this is said and done."

I watched as the smile crept up on her face. She truly believed what she was saying. Even I could tell none of that was true. It'd been a whole week, and she hadn't talked about going home yet. She didn't even want to go home and get clothes. Something more than she was saying was going on. I could waste my time being in her shit, but I had my own to deal with.

Just then, a thought came to me. "Oh, when do you want me to take you home and get you some clothes? You're stretching mine out."

She looked at me like I had her fucked up. "That's funny. You're bigger than me."

"You a damn lie. That dress fits my figure perfectly. In fact, it was made for me. You put it on and stretched it out." I pointed out in a matter of fact tone.

"Anyway, you don't have to take me to my house. I have someone coming to pick me up in the morning." She rolled her eyes, getting off the couch. Silently, I was thanking God. I was also praying that she stayed her ass home. Keyona cleaned up after herself and all. It was just her presence that I couldn't stand. Her whole vibe threw me off.

"Oh, good!" I said a little too excited.

She didn't respond as she got up and went toward the back. Sitting there for a few more minutes, I was playing with my phone. I was debating on calling Lah. I wanted to talk to him, badly. An idea popped into my head. If Lah wasn't going to answer me, I was just going to have to try harder for his attention.

CHAPTER 10

KEN-YONA

It'd been almost a month since I hit Rell upside the head. I felt kind of bad for doing it. If I didn't, he would've found out about my plans. I couldn't have that. I thought faking my pregnancy would have him wanting to marry me sooner. Instead, it had his ass paranoid. What else was I supposed to do?

Then, his nosey ass little sister was in the mix. Hearing the name Tech, I had to act fast or risk it all. I wasn't risking shit. Tech was depending on me to get this money. It wasn't my idea in the first damn place.

He'd been after the Casique family for the whole two years I'd been with Rell. That's how I met Rell in the first place. I was supposed to have set his ass up for Tech to rob. Well, shit didn't work out quite like that.

Tech got knocked some weeks after I started 'dating' Rell. He'd gotten so angry, he beat this dude with the butt of his gun. Dumb ass did it all on camera. Once the police got ahold of him, it was over.

So, while this nigga was in jail, I was stuck with Rell's weak ass. I didn't dare leave, though. Tech had told me to stay with him until he got out. I'm thinking he was getting out in a couple of months. Nope! This nigga was in jail a whole two years!

Honestly, I'd forgotten about his ass. Not like, literally. I just forgot we were setting someone up. By that time, I'd fallen for Rell.

In the beginning of all this, I'd feel bad for doing Rell wrong. Each time he made love to me, I fell deeper and deeper in love with him. Everything about Rell, I fell in love with.

I never had someone treat me as nice as he did. Even though I'd grown up in a well-established home, I still never felt the love from them that Rell gave. He was so attentive. He cared about what I wanted whereas with my family, it was all about 'following family foot steps'. Both my parents were realtors, so they expected me to do the same. Um, I think the fuck not. I didn't want to sell big ass houses. I wanted to live in them. Really, I didn't want to do shit. The only way I could get my parents off my back was to go to school out of state.

Once I'd gotten out of Georgia, I ran free like a naked baby through daisies. I met Tech during my sophomore year at Chicago State. I was intrigued by his demeanor and status. Tech was also a good-looking dude.

He stood at least 6'1 with light hazelnut skin, dark green eyes, dark pink lips, and thick manicured eyebrows. Back then, Tech was a 'pretty nigga'. One of those light skinned niggas with pretty hair.

Tech also had money. After getting knocked, that shit

disappeared with his good-looking appearance. Before he went in jail, he looked like a young thug. Now, he looked like a nigga with the light skin and ugly scars. I will say, his scars and newfound muscles had me swooning on sight.

Tech: *I'm outside, c'mon.*

I looked at the text message I'd just received from Tech. He was going to take me to get some more of my clothes and stuff. I figured Rell wasn't home anyway. He wouldn't know if I'd been there or not. I'd gone by there a few weeks ago, just to see if anyone was home.

To my surprise, nobody was. It didn't look like a soul had stepped in it since the day we left for that bogus ass doctor's appointment.

I walked outside with a hoodie over my head. This has been my routine since I was on the run from Rell. I knew his whole family was on the search and rescue team, looking for me.

"What took you so long?" Tech barked at me the minute I got inside his car. Summer was already here, so it was hot. Tech's car didn't have air conditioning. Add that to the fact I had on a damn hoodie.

"I was looking out the window, damn. When you going to get your stupid air conditioning fixed? It's hot as hell up in here." I complained, snapping my seatbelt on. Tech was a reckless ass driver. The way his temper was set-up, he also had terrible road rage.

"Fuck you looking out the window for? You knew I was coming here to get your scary ass. Had you just listened to me in the first place, you wouldn't be ducking bullets now." Tech barked at me in a harsh tone. No nigga except him and Rell could hurt a bitch feelings and have my ass crying in the passenger seat.

Tech told me not to do 'that weak pregnant shit', as he called it. He warned me that it wouldn't work. Me being me, I didn't listen to his ass. I just knew it would work. It always worked when the girlfriend claimed to be pregnant to keep her man. Why couldn't it work for me? Rell was my man!

"Fuck you, Tech! If it wasn't for me, your ol' stupid ass wouldn't have a fucking come-up now. I stuck by this nigga for two years, for your ass!" I pointed in his face, tears streaming down my face. Usually, I didn't like letting him see me cry or even break a sweat. I didn't care right now, though. I was pissed. He had some nerve throwing shit in my face when all this shit I was doing was for him!

Sure, I fell in love with Rell along the way. That shit died over a year ago. That was right around the time he started putting his family before me. I didn't like coming after anything. It was Keyona before anything.

"Key, I'm sorry. Don't cry, baby. You right. I'm just stressed about not having any money to take care of you. I'm going to do better, baby, I promise." he started pleading his case.

Checkmate, I smirked to myself.

It never failed. All I had to do was start the water-works. It worked on Rell too many times. I think he started to catch on later on in the relationship, though.

It didn't make one difference or another to him, though. He'd still do whatever it was that I wanted from him. See, that's what I loved about him. He cared about me so much, he didn't care if I was faking it or not. He just wanted me. He wanted to take care and love me right.

Thinking about it now made me feel like shit. I'd done a completely innocent man dirty. Rell had the biggest heart, and I fucked him over. If ever he saw me, I knew he'd kill my ass. That is, if he knew I was involved. If I got a chance to see him, I'd turn all this shit on Tech's ass and get my man back.

This time, I'd do so much better. I'd even try and get along with his family for him. IF I got that chance again…

"We're here." Tech pulled up in front of the house. "Aight, so, go in and—"

POP! POP! POP! POP! POP!

"Aghh!" I jumped out the car as I heard bullets start to fly. The smarter thing to do was probably stay my ass in the car and duck. I was so scared, I didn't know what to do.

"Keyona! Get yo stupid ass in the car and let's go!" Tech barked over the bullets.

"Agghh!" I continued to run in circles as the bullets ceased. "Tech! They shooting!"

"No shit, dumb ass! I ain't got no heat on me. You were supposed to go get my gun off layaway, remember?!"

"Aggghh!" I continued to run and scream. The bullets had stopped flying, but I didn't know what to do. I was so scared, I thought I might shit on myself. Thinking fast, I ran toward the house.

Skkkrrr!

Stepping onto the porch, I fished the keys out my pocket. I turned to see if Tech was coming inside. This nigga and the car was gone. Bitch ass nigga left me.

Running inside the house, I slammed the door shut and threw my back against it. My heart was beating a mile a minute, chest heaving up and down. I felt my stomach skip around and ran to the bathroom.

As I leaned over to release the minimum contents of my stomach, I felt pressure on my booty hole as I farted. Oh shit, I was about to shit on myself. Quickly, I turned to sit on the toilet and release everything on that end too. It was sweet relief. I now felt calm and cool.

BOOM! BANG! CREEEK!

I heard a bunch of ruckus out in the living room. That caused me to become more nauseous. I was back to shitting again. I held my hand over my mouth to keep myself from screaming. I was in one of the bathrooms upstairs in the guest rooms. I was praying they didn't find me. Besides me passing gas and shitting, I was quiet.

Dear Lord,

I need you now!

"Little bitch, little bitch, comere!" I heard an unfamiliar voice come near the room I was in. Pressing my hand tighter, I closed my eyes and prayed silently that nobody would find me.

"I hear you, little bitch. You might as well come on out of hiding. I'm going to get you one way or another." the masculine tone grunted, coming near.

Slightly, I lifted my butt to wipe. Pulling my pants up, I struggled to button the jeans I had on. They were Kassidy's. Go figure.

After getting the pants situated, I washed my hands. If I was going to die, I was dying with washed hands after shitting the way I did. Before I had to dry them, the bathroom door swung open.

"Ahh, I found you…aye, Lah!" he yelled behind him. "She in here!"

"Gotdamn! It smells like something died in this bitch!" Rell's brother appeared. This was the one I couldn't stand the most. He was loud, obnoxious, and always had something slick to say. The other brother was quieter. He was also a lot nicer. Despite what that family thought of me, he still spoke. Come to think of it, Tech kind of favored him...

"Isi, please don't kill me!" I shrieked with my wet hands up.

"Calm down, bitch. I'm not here to kill your ass. As much as I want to though. Rell wouldn't allow it." he spoke in a bored tone. Immediately, I broke down crying. Even now, when I could be gunned down by his brother, Rell protected me. I'd done him so dirty and didn't deserve his love or anything. Tech was supposed to be my man. Since he didn't have a gun, he couldn't get his ass out the car. He just left me for dead.

"Thank you, thank you, thank so much." I fell to my knees, crying my heart out. These were real tears. I was so grateful.

"Don't thank me just yet. I don't know what Rell has planned for you." Isi grabbed me by the arm and dragged me out the bathroom. At the mention of Rell's name, I got excited.

"Rell's here? Where is he?" I anxiously inquired. Lah scoffed, but didn't answer me. "Seriously, where's Rell? Y'all going to kill me, huh? I thought you said he said I was off limits?"

"Riley, shut that bitch up." Isi gave the big, burly dude orders and he followed suit. He took the navy-blue bandana off his head and wrapped it around my mouth.

I was quiet for the rest of the ride. I didn't know where

we were going, but the Chicago trees and scenery was starting to fade.

We pulled up to this old run-down building. Looking around the area, it reminded me of something out of *The Hills Have Eyes*. Oh no, these niggas were going to feed me to cannibals or some shit.

Isi got out the car first. Next, the big dude did. He opened my door, but didn't untie my mouth. I guess he didn't want anyone to hear me scream. As if anyone would be able to out here.

He pushed me toward the building until we got to the backdoor. The entire way, I had a bunch of thoughts going through my head. I didn't know what they were going to do with me. They said Rell said not to kill me. That was a relief. So, they couldn't have been going to kill me.

As we walked through the dark building, I heard a tapping noise. It was like a pen being bounced up and down on a desk. The closer we got to it, it was becoming annoying. If it was up to me, I'd scream to it, *shut up*!

"Here she go, bro." Isi pushed me further into the room.

I came face to face with Rell. He didn't have any emotion on his face. It both scared and relieved me. It scared me because I didn't know what he was thinking. I was relieved because I was finally in his presence. Now, I knew for sure Isi and his guard weren't going to touch me.

"Tie her up," Rell said, nonchalantly. My eyes grew big and my heart started pumping faster and harder. I wanted to scream out, protest, beg and cry. It'd be no use. My mouth was covered.

"Take that gag off her mouth," Rell demanded to Isi, and he did as he was told. Gasping, I sucked in as much air as I could.

Rell pulled up a chair. He sat it in front of me and took a seat. I scanned him with my eyes. He looked better than ever. Wearing a black suit, tie, loafers, and his hair freshly faded with a swoosh, Rell was everything. Before, I knew it, but took it for granted. I was only with him because Tech wanted me to. Now, I wished I'd turned on that bastard.

For a few minutes, Rell stared into my eyes. I stared back into his. His eyes weren't the same. They were usually a dark brown. Now, they were like completely black.

"For these past two years, I've given you more than you deserved." He licked his lips after saying that.

"Rell—" I began, but he put his index finger up. Placing it to his lips, he shook his head.

"This isn't the part where you talk, Keyona. This is the part where you listen…" His expression went from blank to angry, then back to blank. It was scary, exorcist-type shit. I didn't know this man sitting in the chair. He wasn't Rell. At least the one I knew…

"Did you ever love me?" he asked, coldly staring into my eyes. I gulped, unsure if I was supposed to talk now. "Answer me!"

I trembled, tears coming down my face. He was now in my face, breathing hot air on me. I hung my head, shaking it. He snatched me by the face, bringing my eyes to stare back into his.

"Answer me, bitch!"

"Yes—" I started to shout yes until he squeezed my cheeks tighter. He had this snarl that spoke volumes. Like, if I lied, he'd kill me where I sat. "N-noo! Rell, I'm sorry!"

I was now sobbing with snot and tears running down my face. Some snot got on Rell's hand. He moved his hand from groping my cheeks. I thought he was going to wipe it on his clothes. Instead, he wiped it on my cheek. I cried harder.

Rell knew how I felt about germs. I didn't care if it was mine or not. This shit was torture. I was bound to a chair. I couldn't move even if I tried. In fact, it seemed like the more I moved, the tighter the chains on my hands were getting. I knew my wrists had to be bleeding by now.

"I gave you everything, Keyona! Everything! Anything you wanted! It was yours! You do me like this?!" I didn't know when or how he managed to get ahold of a photo. He shoved it in my face.

Once it was brought into focus, I noticed it was a picture of me and Tech. He was groping my ass, and I was staring lovingly into his face. Angrily, I squinted at the photo. I was so disgusted with myself for being so stupid.

"Just kill me, Rell. I know that's why you didn't want Isi to do it…" I hung my head, speaking in solemn. I'd stopped crying. What was point? I'd made my bed with the devil. Now, I was going to burn in hell.

"Oh, I will. First, I have to ask you…why'd you lie about being pregnant? Huh? I was going to marry you with or without a baby!" he yelled. When he said that, I looked up. Tears built up to the rim of my eyes. How did he find out about that?

"How did you know?" I asked my thoughts out loud.

Rell was menacingly glaring at me at first. Now, he was smirking. It turned into a laugh. I looked at him like he was a nutcase. I was convinced this wasn't Rell at all.

"I didn't know. You just told me." He stopped laughing, pulling a gun from his waist band and aiming it at me. I took a deep breath, awaiting my death. "I loved you, Keyona…"

POW!

CHAPTER 11

YANNA

Three months later...

"Look, Ms. Yanna! Look what I made you!" This little girl named Sahara came rushing over to me. She was carrying a necklace made of yarn. I smiled at it. She managed to spell my name with orange and black letter beads. She also placed beads shaped like pumpkins and ghosts on it.

"Aww, thank you baby. I love it!" I bent down to hug her. She wrapped her little arms around my body.

Sahara, along with a few others, were my favorites. I was helping a friend of mine with a 'Night Before Halloween' slumber party. She was hosting it for the kids at the community center she owned. It was in the lower parts of Chicago.

She'd invited me a month ago, so I had time to think about it. Being around kids had its pros and cons for me. The pros, I loved being around kids. I lived to see them happy. I was always willing to help them with whatever they needed.

The cons, I loved kids so much it depressed me sometimes. I was struggling to have my own. Being in a room full of them made me want to take one home with me. I knew that'd be the wrong thing to do, though.

As I watched all the kids run around the facility, I imagined my three running with them. That's how many kids I wanted. Kayla named one. However, I wanted two more named after Isi and me. I wanted him to have a Jr., and I wanted my own Jr. I planned on naming her Ayanna instead of Iyanna. This way, we wouldn't get mixed up when people called our names.

"Yanna?" I heard someone call my name. Coming out of my thoughts, I turned my head slightly.

"Sade. Hey, girl!" I cheerfully greeted her.

"Hey, boo. How are you?" She kissed me on the cheek. I did the same thing, kissing her on the cheek.

"I'm good, and you? How's the babies?"

Sade had three. She had two boys and a girl. Her daughter could pass as her twin. Her sons looked like a mixture between her and her husband, Kendrick. Nonetheless, they were a beautiful family.

"They are good. They're somewhere around here, running around. Can you believe the turnout? I didn't think so many parents would allow their kids to come to the slumber party. They hear about their kids staying in a building overnight and be ready to call the police."

I doubled over, cracking up at her silly ass. "Girl! I'm telling you. They don't play about their kids. Shit, I know I wouldn't!"

"Okaaay!" She put her hands up to slap five. I was

laughing but managed to unite my hand with hers. "So, What's up with you and Isi? You have to bun in the oven yet?"

She reached out to rub my stomach. I moved away before she could touch it. I didn't want to appear rude, but I didn't want her feeling on my stomach. There wasn't nothing in it to feel. Her touching it would only bring emotions out of me I didn't need to deal with right now. I shook my head and weakly smiled. Sade's eyes filled to the rim with tears. Now, I felt bad for coming across rude.

"Oh Yanna, I'm so sorry." Her tears fell. She came over and hugged me.

"Thank, you...why are you apologizing?" I was truly confused now. She swiped her tears, scanning the center. I guess she found who she was looking for. She waved the person over. Next, a young lady jogged over to us.

"Yes, boss lady?" she asked in a chipper tone. She couldn't be no more than eighteen.

"Hey, Serenity. Can you and Zach watch the kids while I go to my office for a few minutes? Ryan and Redd are in the TV room getting the movie stuff set up. They'll help y'all too," Sade told her. Serenity nodded her head, keeping her chipper attitude.

"Okay, boss lady!" she smiled, getting ready to walk away.

"Ms. Serenity, come look at the makeover we gave Zachy!" Sahara pranced over.

She had an eyebrow pencil and lipstick in her hands with a huge smile on her face. Serenity got a laugh in before heading over. Sade took me by the hand and led me to her office.

"Sade, what's going on? Why are you crying, girl?" I searched her face with solemn and confusion.

"Girl, I'm so sorry. Why you didn't tell me you miscarried?!" she gasped, crying harder. I backed away from her with my mouth dropped into an O. How did she…

"How did you know I had a miscarriage?" I asked my thoughts out loud. Again, she was wiping her tears.

"The way you moved when I went to playfully touch your stomach. It was all in your face too. I could just tell something happened. Plus, my best friend suffered so many miscarriages, she hated for me to touch her stomach." she explained.

I backed all the way up, not paying attention to my surroundings. My legs bumped into something. Looking down, I noticed it was a sofa and plopped down. I threw my head into my hands and shook my head. I didn't realize I'd made it so obvious.

"Sade…" I started to talk but lost the battle with my tears. "I'm sorry…"

"No, no, no, it's fine. Let your tears out, boo. It's okay to cry." She snatched a couple of Kleenex off her desk and then came to sit next to me.

I took the Kleenex, wiped, and then blew my nose. I'd never talked to anybody about my miscarriage except Isi. He was the only person I cared to share my feelings with. Plus, it was his child too. He wanted me to see someone, but I didn't need any of that. I used reading, cooking, and going out with my girls as a distraction.

Most days, that worked. Others, it didn't. Still, I kept a smile on my face and hope in my heart. I was going to have a baby—naturally, with my husband! I just knew it in my heart that I was.

I didn't care what the doctors said. I didn't care about Isi's doubts either. I told him to find his faith. We were going to have a damn baby!

"Shhh...it's alright, love. Get it all out." Sade continued to soothe me, rubbing my back.

I continued to cry until I was hiccupping. I had a massive headache. It was so bad I couldn't see straight. Laying back against the couch, I put my hand on my head.

"I haven't cried like that since my mother died." I shook my head.

The day my mother died my whole life came crumbling down. At least, I thought it did. I was grateful she got to meet Isi.

She adored him so much, she gave her stamp of approval. When she died, he was there every step of the way for me. He never, not once, left my side. He put all his street dealings to the side for me. That's one of the reasons I'll do anything for that man. I'll always take his side and stand by him. It was *Us Before Anything*.

"I understand, boo. We all go through things. It's not good to hold them in, though. You have to let it out or else everything will build up. Have you talked to anybody about it?" she inquired in a nurturing tone. There was something about women with kids. They had this tone, like it was 'an extra set of patience' type of tone.

I shook my head no. "I don't think I need to talk to anyone about it. I talked to my husband enough. We're getting through it together. Right now, we're trying for another baby," I let her in a little of my business.

"If you don't mind me saying...I think you should talk to someone besides him. You guys should do it together. Like couple's therapy, but baby therapy. I can recommend a group or therapist y'all can go see together..." She smiled. I smiled at her, nodding. I wasn't too sure about seeing a therapist, but I'd give it some thought and talk to Isi about it.

Sade wrote some numbers and names down. After, she passed the paper to me. I read it over with a quick glance. There were all types of doctor's numbers, specialists, and therapy groups. They were so many different outlets to help us get through our tragedy together.

Honestly, I thought we were doing fine. With the way I just broke down from holding it all in, I knew we weren't. Lord knew how much Isi was holding in. I felt bad now. I'd basically told my husband to suck it up, shut up, and get me pregnant.

After talking a little more to Sade, she left the office to let me pull myself together. Pushing the baby business to the back of my mind, I was ready to get back out there and have some fun.

❦

The next morning, I was helping a group of kids get their things together. We had to have them ready by eleven in the morning. The parents were supposed to come get them no later than noon.

After getting the last child ready, I went to go find Sade. I found her in her office. She was sitting behind her desk, looking down at her phone.

Knock, knock,

"Yanna, hey, come in." She looked up from what she was doing. Slowly, I walked in and took a seat. "What's up, boo?" She set her phone down to give me her undivided attention.

"I just want to thank you for yesterday. You were right. I thought I had everything all figured out. It turns out I'm still hurting. I feel like if I have a baby, it'll get rid of the pain." I confessed as reality hit me.

This whole time, I've been hiding my pain from my loved ones. I've been trying to get pregnant to fill the void of losing a child when really, that was impossible. Of all people, I should've known you can't use physical things to block out pain. I took all this psychology in college and was just letting it go over my head.

That was another thing I wanted to talk to Sade about. I'd been sitting on my degree more than two years and hadn't put it to use. I could've been a social worker, counselor, or something in that nature. The truth is, I was too afraid to go into what I really wanted to.

Being around kids consistently, it made me want one more than anything. The thought of not being able to have one scared me. I also loved the kids. It took Sade inviting me to the center to help with the kids for me to realize I was missing out on what I truly loved.

"It was no problem, boo. I'm glad I was able to help you sort things out." She smiled lovingly at me. "Yanna, if I may ask…are you currently working for anyone?"

"No. Other than helping my husband run the family businesses, I'm not doing anything. I have a degree in social science and minored in psychology, though." I explained a little of my credentials to her.

Sade licked her lips and scooted away from desk, getting up. "I asked because I wanted to offer you a position here at Friendship. Yanna, you're so great with the kids. I was watching you with some of them last night. They love you so much."

"Oh wow, Sade...wow..." I was speechless. I couldn't believe she was offering me a job. I was just about to ask her about a job. I wanted to work in the counseling division. I wasn't even sure if they had one.

Just from talking to the kids here, I knew some of them could use someone other than their parents to talk to. Only I'd work with them on helping them get out of tough situations. Anything dealing with their lives at home, school, or personal. Some kids only felt comfortable talking to an adult they'd never met. Sometimes, talking to your parents was uncomfortable. It was nerve racking. You were constantly afraid that they wouldn't believe you, or they'd blame you for the things going on in your life. I wanted to be that one person to make a difference in their lives.

"I know I kind of just sprung this on you. We're looking for someone to work in the counseling division. We need someone who'll be responsible and make the kids their first priorities. I believe you are it. Yanna, I believe that God places us with the right people at the right time. You're in the right place."

I felt shudders as she was speaking. Like, an out of body experience. Her words touched me, and I was tongue tied. Tears welled up along the rims of my eyes. I sucked in a deep breath, letting it out. The tears followed.

"Thank you so much, Sade." I cried.

She came from around the desk and took a seat next to me. Once again, she was pulling me into her arms and hugging me tightly. This lasted for another two minutes. Pulling myself together, I looked into her big, dark brown orbs.

Sade was truly a beautiful woman. Her complexion always reminded me of a dark chocolate candy bar. She reminded of the actress Tika Sumpter.

"So, will you accept the job?"

"Will I? Are you serious? Yes! I would love to work here with you and everyone else. Y'all are so dope!" I couldn't help the tears pouring from my eyes.

"Yass! Okay, great! When do you want to start?" She got up and went back around her desk. She was typing something on her computer.

I sat thinking, ready to answer her question. Then, it hit me. I hadn't even talked to Isi about it. I knew he'd say to take the job. He'd be so excited that I was finally doing something I went to school for. This was what he'd rather have me doing than out hitting the streets with him.

"Umm, actually…let me get back to you on that."

She looked away from her computer with a knowing look. As if we were thinking the same thing, we spoke at the same time. "*Husbands*."

"Girl, yasss!" we exclaimed in unison and laughter at the same time.

"Okay, boo. I can respect that. I don't make life-changing decisions without Kendrick knowing too."

I nodded in complete understanding. "Yup! It's the way of life."

I had to laugh at the thought. I used to think it was weird and unnecessary to have to ask your spouse for permission to do something. I thought it was a controlling mechanism—a power trip. Now that I'm married, I wouldn't do a thing without talking it over with my husband first. He comes first, as do I with him.

"Girl! I know it. Let me finish getting my kids ready to

go." She stood back up. This time, she had a computer bag on her shoulder.

"Okay, boo." I hugged her one more time before going our separate ways.

On my way out the center, I was in the middle of texting Isi the good news. I was so focused on our texting I didn't realize the little girl sitting on the steps until I almost tumbled over her. It was a good thing I kept my balance.

"Oh no, sweetie. I'm so sorry! I didn't mean to bump you like that." Tossing my phone into my bag, I swung it over my shoulder to help the little girl. Her belongings were scattered on the steps.

After getting everything ready for her, I set her bag down next to her. She hadn't spoken since we almost fell over each other. Giving her a once over, I noticed she had on some blush pink leggings and a white ruffled shirt with a few spots on it. She was also wearing a pair of black dress shoes with no socks. Her head was down in her knees, so I couldn't look at her face. I noticed her hair was in a big poof, though.

"Hi, sweetie. Are you alright?" I kneeled to her level. Automatically, I smelled the stench of urine on her. It almost knocked me out, making me fall the rest of the way down the steps.

She still didn't say anything. She was sniffling, like she was crying. I noticed the tears from her eyes hitting the pavement.

"Hey, baby girl. My name is Iyanna. I work here at the center. I just want to make sure you alright. Are you waiting for your mother?" I softened my tone. Hearing myself lie about working at the center sounded surreal. I had to speak it and claim it into existence.

"She…" the little girl started to say, but then choked on her words and began to sob harder.

"Aww, shh…it's going to be alright, baby." I pulled her into my arms and rocked her back and forth. I began to pray for her. I didn't know this little girl from a can of paint. I had no idea why she was crying. All I could think to do was pray.

Once she gathered herself, she pulled away from me. Staring up into my eyes, her plump pink bottom lip poked out. I smiled, looking down at her pretty, soft light brown face. Noticing the bluish-purple bruise, I looked closely at it. It appeared to be fresh, like it was recently put there. A part of me wanted to reach out and touch baby girl's face. I wanted to see if she was in pain from her bruises. I also didn't want to scare her, so I kept my hands to myself.

"What's your name, pretty girl?" I asked her in a calm tone. She sniffled before answering me.

"Ayanna Dalton." She hiccupped.

"A—" my voice got stuck in my throat as I put my hand over my mouth. Tears welled up in my eyes. She had the exact same name I wanted to name one of my daughters. *Okay, pull yourself together Yanna*, I coached myself.

"Ayanna, hi sweetie. My name is *Iyanna* Casique." I held my hand out for her to shake. She was slow to take it but did it anyway.

"Hi." Weakly, she smiled at me. Watching the corners of her lips turn up moved my heart. It made me feel tingly inside.

I only felt like this when I was around Isi. He was my love. I was in love with him. It was crazy/weird to feel this way about someone else—a little girl I didn't even know. Why did I feel this way?

"Where are your parents, baby girl?" I quizzed. I knew something was off the minute I spotted her on the steps. Come to think of it, I didn't remember seeing her at the sleepover either. She must've just arrived this morning.

"Um, my mama brought me here. She told me to stay here at this building. Then, she just left. I asked her where she was going. She said that she had to go. She was shaking a lot. She was crying."

"How old are you?" I quizzed with squinted eyes. From the look and sound of her face and voice, I assumed she was young. She couldn't be but five or six.

"Seven." she lowly spoke.

"*Seven*." I whispered, pulling her in for a hug. This baby was only seven. The way she explained her mother leaving her on some steps blew me. No seven-year-old should have to go through this.

"Okay sweetheart. Umm…come with me." I stood up with my hand out to her. She stared my hand with uncertainty. I could sense she was scared. "It's okay. I'm going to take you inside. We're going to get you some food and it'll be okay, okay?"

Ayanna looked as if she was weighing out her options. I waited two more minutes until she slowly nodded her head. She then took my hand.

Leading her into the building, we bumped into Sade. She was holding both her son and daughter's hand. Weakly, I smiled at them. They were so beautiful, picture perfect together.

"Yanna?" Sade looked from me and then to Ayanna with a confused expression.

"Sade, hey. I know you're about to close, but um…" I held Ayanna's small hand up as recognition. She looked at the little girl, sadness embedding her face. Her hand went to her mouth as the tears began to fall freely down her face.

"Yeah, yeah, come on baby." Sade took her by the hand and led her toward the back. I stood there, not knowing what to do next.

My heart was heavy from just being around the little girl. I couldn't place my finger on it, but Sade seemed to know this child. As I stood deep in thought, the sound of her heels click-clacking my way caught my attention.

"Hey." She hung her head with her arms folded over her chest.

"Hey, who is that little girl?" I asked the million-dollar question.

"Umm, her name is Ayanna Dalton. She's been coming to the center since she was five. Her mother usually just drops her off on the steps and just…leaves. She stopped coming a few months ago. I've been praying for the day I saw her again. I was so worried about her. Ayanna's mother isn't…" Sade shook her head with sadness in her eyes.

She didn't have to say anything else. It didn't take a rocket scientist to figure out Ayanna's mother wasn't right in the mind. I mean, who leaves their child on the steps in front of a damn building? Thinking about it was sickening.

"Wow…" I blew out a breath. "She told me her mom left her on the steps this morning. She said she was shaking and crying. She told her to stay on the stairs and that's it."

"*She's at it again…*" Sade shook her head.

"So, what do we do?" I eagerly asked.

"I'm going to take her home with me. I'll get in contact with social services in the morning. For now, I want to make sure she gets a hot bath, clean clothes, and a good meal."

I nodded my head with a reassuring smile. I didn't blame Sade. I would've done the exact same thing. My only prayer was that Ayanna was safe, and God placed her where she needed to be.

CHAPTER 12

ISI

Knock, knock,

"Come in," Pops answered from the other side of his office. Opening the door, I walked in. I felt a strong breeze circle around my body. Pops had every window opened in the joint.

"Aye, Pops. You wanted to see me?" I asked, taking my time entering the room.

I couldn't stand being cold. I didn't care too much for being warm either, though. This nigga loved air. He'd turn on every fan, air condition, and opened every window, just to be cool.

"What's up, son? Have a seat." He didn't even look up at me. He just knew it was one of his sons. I took a seat in the chair in front of his desk. "I'll be right with you," he said, his head still down and doing whatever it was that he was doing.

I felt my phone vibrate in my pocket. Pulling it out, I saw a text from my baby. She was letting me know she was busy at home cooking for me.

That got me riled up. I loved Yanna's cooking. Truth be told, sometimes it was better than Ma's and Mama's. They could burn and everything. So, well, I didn't think I'd meet anyone that could top their food. I was wrong. Yanna had them beat. Of course, I'd never tell them that.

"I'm sorry about that, son. I had to make some last-minute calls on one of the loaners. Do you know this nigga been owing money since January? I only gave him a slap on the wrist because I thought I could trust him." He placed his hand over face.

I hated to see him so stressed. For that reason alone, I took on a lot of the tasks at the office. I was turning into a baby Pops. I knew my wife was wondering what I was always doing on the phone. Shit, half the time, I even wondered. Pops had big shoes to fill.

"Pops, you know the drill. Trust no nigga except your own." I used his own words on him. All the things he instilled into me and my brothers growing up, he should've known better.

"The nigga is my cousin. Twice removed, but family either way." He laughed it off. I scoffed, smiling at his joke. Let Pops tell it, he was the funniest nigga in the world. I laughed to make him feel good about his humor.

I didn't know what to say about his cousin doing him wrong. I didn't have those types of problems. Pops never gave us the keys on how to deal with backstabbing family members. Forgive them…I suppose…

"Let's get to why I got you here, though…" He cleared his throat.

Finally, I thought to myself as I slouched a little in the chair, I was in.

I was ready to be home with my sexy wife. Between

giving orders and taking them, I was burnt out for the day. I was next up to run the businesses. That wasn't going to happen until Pops felt he was ready to retire. The way things were looking now, this nigga would be dust before that happened.

"Have you been looking into this situation with Tech?" he asked in a hushed tone. As if we were being recorded. Shit, messing with Ma, we probably were.

Pops had given me the rundown on who Tech was to him. I was the only one besides Ma who he told. He only told me because I was the oldest. He said the others wouldn't get it.

Before he got with Ma, he was with Tech's moms. He had a lot of love for her, but he wasn't in love with her. He was just young and doing him. She was his main dip.

He'd go to her when he was hungry or wanted to fuck. He said sometimes, he'd stash drugs in her crib too.

Anyway, once he met Ma, he wanted to dead things with anybody he messed with before. In fact, Ma demanded it. Pops respected her authority. He loved that she respected herself enough to know she wasn't sharing a nigga with no other bitch.

The night he went to break shit off with Tech's mama, he ended up breaking her off her last taste of his dick. He didn't hear from her after that day.

A year later, when Ma had just got pregnant with me, ol' girl reached out. She claimed she had a kid, and it was his. Pops didn't believe it, so he ignored her. He never told Ma like he should've, either.

Once Ma pushed me out and a year went by, ol' girl was still reaching out. She sent pictures and everything. Pops said he finally looked at them. The kid looked like me, or I looked like him. The only difference, Tech had green-looking eyes like his mother.

By that time, Pops still hadn't said a thing to Ma about it. He kept it a secret. He planned to take the shit to his grave. That is, until his long-lost son came looking for him.

It'd been three months since Rell killed Keyona's snake ass. Tech still hadn't shown up. We were on the search, but nothing was coming up. Now, this nigga wanted to hide.

My idea was to let his ass stay wherever he was. He wouldn't be there for long if he had motive. That's when we'd get his ass.

I wasn't sure what Pops' plan was next. He could either take him in or…you know…I don't even want to say that shit. After all, he was my big brother. Enemy right now or not, he was family. It was *Us Before Anything*.

"Isi…" Pops waved his hands in my face, grabbing my attention. I shook my head from my thoughts.

"We still got nothing, Pops," I answered his question. "I think we should chill on the search. Let him come to us. He don't want to be found, Pops."

He nodded his head in agreement. "I hear you, son. I just want to find him…this shit is my fault. I should've been there for him."

I shook my head. I hated that he was beating himself up. When he first told me the story, I was heated. After talking it over with my baby, she got me to calm down. She then explained things from Pops' point of view of things. She helped me let that shit go. Yanna, man…that was my baby, my rib, my backbone, my everything. A lot of shit, I don't think I'd get through without her.

"Pops, you have to let go. You can't keep beating yourself up. It happened. Now, it's time to face the music. You have to make shit right with ol' dude." I gave him the best advice I could, given his circumstances.

"I hear you. I just wish your mother would talk to me. You know I ain't had no pussy in a month? She ain't even cooking for me no more. Mama's ass somewhere busy puffing cigaweed to feed her son." He pouted in his chair. I smirked, trying not to laugh. I couldn't say I knew where he was coming from. Shit, I didn't even know if I had sympathy.

Ma was doing right. She was pissed. So pissed, she was taking it out on us all. He's complaining about him not getting no meals. We were suffering every Sunday now because of his ass. Because he wanted to 'break a bitch off' as a farewell present.

"A nigga getting fat from eating junk and fast food. Son, I got blue balls! Blue balls, son!" he exclaimed. That was my cue. I stood up to leave.

"Too much info, Pops." I chuckled.

"Blue balls, son! Blue balls!" He threw at my back on my way out the office. I was cracking my ass up. That's what he gets!

"Bye, Pops. Love you!" I called over my shoulder before leaving.

I heard him say it back, but not as cheerful as I did. Old mad ass!

When I got home, I could already smell what my wife made me for dinner. My favorites: fried fish, cornbread, and spaghetti. Setting my computer bag down near the door, I headed to the kitchen.

She had R-Kelly bumping in the background. My baby was trying to get something started. We'd been going at it like rabbits, trying to make a baby these past few months. I knew she was trying to set the right mood so we could go round for round.

I loved that her confidence about conceiving was boosted. Before, she was doubting it. I was the one doubting it now. Just like that, the tables turned. I didn't lose complete faith. I just didn't have as much as I did before.

Yanna told me to stop overthinking it. She said we weren't giving up, and for me to find my faith. I remember telling her those exact words. Since the miscarriage, she'd gained confidence. She looked at it as a sign that if she could miscarry, she could conceive. If she could conceive, she could carry a baby.

Making my way through the house, I found Yanna standing near the stove. She was leaning against the counter, sipping a glass of white wine. She loved white wine. She never drank too much of it because she always got a headache later.

"Hey, beautiful." I went over and placed kisses along her jawline, neck to her collarbone.

"Mmm, hey daddy. I missed you all day…" She moaned-slurred. That told me she'd drank plenty of wine. Taking the empty glass from her, I set it on the counter and then picked her up. Carrying her to the island in the middle of the kitchen, I placed her on top of it.

Engaging in a kissing session for a few minutes, I let my hands roam freely all over her body. My baby was groping and pulling against me roughly. I could taste the amount of wine on her tongue. She must've had a hard day.

Yanna only drank wine excessively if she was having one of those days. That was usually when her period came, or she was feeling some type of way. It wasn't her period this time around. That'd passed already, so she'd had a bad day.

"I missed you more, baby. What's up with you? How was your day?" Pulling away, I stared into her eyes. I searched them for answers and found sadness. Her eyes welled up to the rim with tears. Now, I had different emotions surging through me. When my babe hurt, I hurt. I didn't even know what was bothering her, but I felt it circulating my loins.

"Isi…" she whispered, allowing the tears to disperse her eye sockets.

"Baby, what's wrong?" I hugged her close and tightly.

She was now crying in the crook of my neck, holding me tighter. She had both her arms and legs wrapped around me. It was like a leech, stuck to your skin. I didn't mind, though. If this was comforting her, I would stand here for however long she needed.

She shook her head, tears escaping her face. I wiped each one away as they continued to come down. "Today, I met a little girl at the community center. She was lost and just…broken. When I asked her where her mother was, she told me she left her on the steps at the center…"

Sucking in a deep breath, she tried to compose herself. I stayed by her side, rubbing her back in silence.

"It broke my heart, babe. Here's a little girl with nowhere to go. She doesn't know where her next meal will come from. All because her mother didn't want her. Lord knows how bad I want a child. What I'd do if I had one. Seeing her today just took a lot out of me."

"Where is she now?" I inquired, compassion filling me up.

"She went with Sade. She took her home with her for the night. She knows who the little girl is and her mother…I don't know what's going to happen to her."

I took a deep breath in and out. I was more than relieved to hear that Sade had the girl. Sade and her husband, Kendrick, were good people. Back when we were running the streets heavy, we used to link up often. He was now retired along with his right-hand, Zay.

"All we can do is pray, babe. It's going to be alright," I assured her.

"You're right baby. I'm just worried about her. I wish you could've met her. She's only seven years old."

I studied the look in her eyes for a moment. My wife just met this little girl and seemed taken by her. I knew it was eating at her that she couldn't do anything to help the girl.

"You ever think about putting your degree to use? You know, getting out there and making a difference for these kids?"

Her head shot up and eyes widened. "That's actually what I wanted to talk to you about next. Sade offered me a job. I would've taken it on the spot—I almost did, actually. I wanted to see what you thought first."

"I think you should accept the offer. You know how I feel about you pursuing your dreams. Honestly, when you decided not to do social work, I felt bad. Like maybe it my fault. You were so caught up in the game with me and didn't have to be."

She nodded. "I know, babe. It wasn't your fault, though. I didn't want to start my career working with kids because I felt I couldn't have any. The thought of being around them in hostile environments scared me. Now, today, being around all the kids...hearing them call my name in excitement. Working with them and listening to them...I know this is where I belong."

Hearing my wife talk about her passion and career put a smile on my face. I loved that she wanted to get back to what she went to school for. I couldn't count how many times I told her to get back into it. Thank God she wanted to now.

"I'm happy you're taking this step, mama. You already know I'm right here with you. Just say the word, ma. You stayed down with me and didn't have to. Anything you want or need you know you got that. I love and appreciate everything you do, baby."

"I love you too, Isiah. I also want to apologize to you for putting all this pressure on you about having a baby. It was selfish and unfair to you. I just wanted a baby so bad. After the miscarriage, I felt so empty. I thought the only way to replace the feeling of losing a child was having another one. I know now that I can't do that."

Listening to the words coming out her mouth, I couldn't help or stop the tears coming from my eyes. Pulling her into my arms, I rocked her in an embrace. I had no idea she'd been feeling this way.

Thank you, God, I thanked the man above.

"I love you, baby. We're going to get through this together, okay? One day at a time."

"I love you too. We are going to get through this. I know just how." She pulled away, searching my eyes.

"How?"

She held her hands out. I placed mine in hers. Closing her eyes and bowing her head, I followed suit.

"Father God, thank you for blessing us to see another day together. We're forever grateful and know that you are powerful over all things. Lord, we need you now more than anything. We're broken and need to be fixed. We know that it's going to take a lot of work and faith. As long as we have each other and you, we can get through this. In Jesus name, Amen."

"Amen."

CHAPTER 13
KAS

Inside my car, I sat outside of his building. Looking in my compact mirror, I popped my lips to make sure my lipstick was on point. It was. So was my eyeliner, eyelashes, and mascara. Stepping out my car, the downtown Chicago breeze hit my bare thighs and cleavage.

This time, I was wearing clothes. I planned on leaving in clothes as well. I'd pressed out my 24' Peruvian lace front. I had on a soft pink shirt with a crisscross opening, showing off my bare titties. The shorts I wore were specially made for me too. Well, at least they fit my body like they were. It was like they were glued around my ass and hips, showing off my meaty thighs. On my feet were a pair of black open toed, four-inch sandals.

I entered the building and noticed there was a different receptionist. It was a man I'd never seen. He was an older gentleman with gray hair on his head, beard, and mustache.

"Welcome to the Mirabella, ma'am. What can I do for

you?" he greeted me with a smile and kind tone. *This should be a piece of cake*, I thought to myself.

"Umm, yea. I'm here to visit my boyfriend. He told me to ask the front desk for his access code so I can just come up." I lied with a perfect smile. I'd never seen him here before. I figured he may've been new. "When did you start working here?"

"I started the other day, ma'am." He smiled.

"Aww! Well…" I searched for his name badge. "*Jeffery*, you're doing a wonderful job."

He blushed and chuckled. "Why thank you, ma'am."

"You're so welcome." I held the plastic smile. The best way to get on anyone's good side was to make some talk and tell them they were doing a great job, even if they were completely bombing it.

"Who are you here to see?" he asked me, bringing me back to why I'd come in the first place.

"His name is Lah Casique." I told him. Lah had never told me if his real name was Lah or something else. I was kind nervous and feeling ashamed now. I hope that got me by.

"Okay, yes. You're here to see Mr. Casique. You must be his girlfriend, Kori." He cheerfully smiled at me. My smile dropped at the mention of Kori.

I knew I'd heard that bitch's voice in the background! Then, Jeffery just revealed that she was his 'girlfriend'. No bitch, I was his girlfriend!

"Ms. Bryant?" Jeffery called out.

"Who?" I looked at him sideways.

"I'm sorry. Would you prefer to be called Kori instead of Ms. Bryant?" he asked in concern. Shaking my head, I remembered I was supposed to be in character. I noticed he was holding a small square piece of paper out to me.

I grabbed it and balled it up. "Umm, Kori is fine. Oh, and Jeffery, if a woman comes by here saying she's Kori Bryant, kick her out. She's super obsessed with me and Mr. Casique's relationship."

Jeffery was making faces. His expressions were going from shocked to confused to concern. "Oh no, Ms. Kori. Do you have a description, picture or something?"

I smiled, anxious to get to my phone. Once I found the picture of Kori on her profile, I showed it to Jeffery. He rapidly nodded. After that was done, I headed up to Lah's penthouse.

When I entered, it appeared empty. The light was on in the living room and kitchen, though. I wasn't sure if Lah was here or not. I wanted to call out his name. Then again, I didn't want to alarm him. I wanted to surprise him. He hadn't seen me in a few weeks, so it'd be unexpected.

Quietly, I walked toward the back where his room was. The light was on and the bed was covered in rose petals. I noticed a platter with different fruits, wine, cheese and massage oils. There was also slow music playing, filling up the room. *Aww, he had a special night planned then, huh? Is that Jagged Edge?*

*Meet me at the altar in your white dress. We ain't getting no younger. We might as well do this...*I hummed and danced along to the music. I was feeling the rhythm so much, I began to strip my clothes off. I heard the shower stop just as I was crawling on top of the bed. Lah was going to come out the shower to me lying naked on his bed.

"Baby, is that you?" I heard the familiar feminine tone. She was calling out from the bathroom.

Just then, I heard the elevator doors open and close with a *ding*. "Baby? You here?"

It was Lah. Kori answered, still in the bathroom. "Yeah baby! I'm in the bedroom!"

Bitch don't be talking like this your shit. Like you live here or something, I scoffed to myself.

"Aight, come here. I want to show you something," he called her to the front. Thinking fast, I gathered my clothes and rushed into his walk-in closet. I heard her swiftly walk by and out the room. I peeked my head out the closet entrance to see where they were in the house.

I was nervous because I had to figure out an escape plan. Walking back into the closet, I paced around, nervously. I was low-key praying that God got me out this penthouse. If Lah walked in and saw me, there's no telling what he might do.

As I backed further into his closet, my heart raced as their voices got closer. Kori was doing a lot of moaning and giggling Lah's name. That bitch was calling my man daddy.

Pulling his clothes back, I prepared myself to hide in his clothes. I was going to hide for as long as they were in this penthouse. If that meant I was spending the night in this closet, so be it.

As I crouched down low in his clothes near his shoes, I spotted a small door. It wasn't so small that a human being couldn't get through it. What if it was a way leading out of the building? I was a little nervous to open it. What if it set off an alarm or creaked as I opened it. Kori and Lah would know I was in here.

Saying fuck it, I went ahead and prayed for the best. I placed my hand on the knob and pulled against the door.

Turning the knob, I began to slowly open the door. So far, so good. Once it was fully open, I stepped inside. I realized it was a bunch of flights of stairs.

I took the flights all the way down and got to another door. There was an exit sign above the entrance. I pushed the door open and was out the building.

All I could do was thank God because I dodged a bullet —literally. Lah might've shot my ass. Now, I had to figure out how to get rid of this bitch Kori.

🌀

Click.

I was on my way, rushing back to my car when I heard a gun cock. I knew it was a gun because I'd heard the same noise the night I was arrested at Lah's. The police had threatened to shoot if I didn't calm down. There were like four officers. They were cocking and drawing their guns at me. If you never been in that sort of situation, the shit is nerve racking. You'll do whatever it takes to make it out alive.

"Move another muscle and you're dead, bitch." I heard a deep masculine voice say from behind me. Immediately, I grew afraid. Did Lah somehow figure out it was me? I was so scared, I wasn't even trying to make out the voice.

"Please. I'm sorry. I shouldn't have been inside your house. Nor should I have told the doorman I was Kori. I'm sorry. Please, don't kill me, Lah." I begged through tears.

"Bitch—" he said, then halted himself. He then jerked me around roughly. "This ain't Lah!"

It was dark, but I could see him clear as day. He was

the same skin tone as Lah. He had lips like his and every-thing. The only difference and what distinguished him from my man was that his eyes were a greenish color. Lah's were dark brown and sexy. His eyes were sexy as well. Just not as sexy as Lah's.

"W-who are y-you?" I stuttered out between deep breaths.

"My name isn't important. All you need to know is that I've been watching you." he admitted. For some reason, hearing him confess that he'd been stalking me didn't scare me at all.

"Why have you been following me?"

"Because you're after the same thing I am." he answered in a calm manner.

I stared at him, dumbfounded. "And what's that?"

"The Casique family…"

"The who? No, I'm not. You're mistaken. I'm only after my man. I don't know about this family you speak of."

"Well, your man is a part of that family, and you're going help me."

"Help you what?" I trembled in fear.

"Kill them…" he spoke with much confidence.

Oh hell no. I didn't want Lah *this* bad. "What makes you think I'll help you do a such thing? Who are you to them? Why do you want them dead?"

"None of that is any of your business."

"All you need to know is that you're going to help me."

"W-what if I-I don't?" I feared the answer, yet I asked anyway.

"You'll die too."

"I—"

Bink!

All I saw was stars before everything went black. *Dear Lord, if you help me get out this one, I promise I'll leave Lah alone for good.*

CHAPTER 14

RELL

I was just wrapping up a meeting with Isi, Pops, and a new potential client when Rizz shot me a text. She wanted to meet up at my house. She said she was bringing Chinese food. That alone told me all I needed to know. She was upset about something.

Lately, things between us were good. I enjoyed the feeling of us just being friends and nothing extra. I'd been seeing a therapist every other week. She thought it was a good idea if I didn't see Rizz at all. I told her she was out her rabid ass mind. I wasn't paying her to give me bad advice.

Rizz was my best friend. In love or not, I wasn't giving that up ever again. I allowed Keyona to come between it the first time. Nothing or no one was coming between it this time.

Not even Rizz's nigga. I did agree to give her some space and let her breathe. I'd started seeing this therapist for one sole reason. After all that shit with Keyona, my head was gone. I couldn't get over how wrong she did me.

I mean, she really fooled a nigga. Thank God for my family because Lord knows what I would've done, or where I would've been.

Knock, knock.

"Come in," I called out with my back turned. I was busy packing my briefcase to leave for the day. Rizz said she'd be at my house in an hour.

"Hey, bro." It was Liz. Turning with my briefcase in my hand, I faced her.

She was dressed in an all-white suit with red lipstick and heels. She was even wearing her hair down for a change. It was a different look for her, yet it looked good on her.

"Hey, baby sis. What's up?"

"You remember when you asked me to check in on Rizz's nigga…John, right?" she smirked. She knew the nigga's name. I appreciated what she was trying to do, though.

"Sis, cut the bullshit. I ain't worried about ol' boy. He makes Rizz happy. That's all that matters to me." I smiled wholeheartedly.

I meant everything I just said. It took me a little minute to see it, but I was tripping. I mean, I'd heard of niggas going coo-coo from one whiff of the right pussy. I never took that shit serious, though. After Rizz and I started having sex, I found out how true it was. It was like I was addicted or some shit. Once I came to my senses, I realized I was acting out of character.

"So, if I give you this folder full of all his dirt, you won't care to look?" she asked with a raised eyebrow, her chin tilted and lips pursed to the side.

"Honestly, no. Actually, I wish I never had you spying

on dude. I mean, it's none of my business. Rizz feeling him, I'm good." I shrugged. I watched Liz's face drop in suspicion.

"Umm, like a few months ago, you were all against dude. You swore you were kidnapping her and forcing her to marry you. What changed?"

I laughed because she was right. I was ready to go to jail for holding Rizz hostage as my wife. I was on some Dre shit from *Doing The Most For My Thug* by Shanah Little. Shit, I was 'doing the most' alright.

"I'm just in a different place than before."

"So, you don't want to be with Rizz anymore?" she asked, her voice cracking like she was going to cry. For a minute, I searched her eyes for any signs of tears.

"Of course, I do. I just want her to want to be with me too. Right now, we're building our friendship back up. I'm cool with that for now. Plus, Dr. Herguth said to let things come naturally. So, I am."

Liz scrunched her face up. "You're still seeing the shrink?"

"Yeah, actually I am."

"I thought you stopped seeing her. You said she asked too many questions and tried to get you admitted in a psych ward." she pointed out. Everything she was saying was true, except the part about the psych ward. Dr. Herguth did ask way too many questions, though.

"Nigga, you know damn well that was y'all. Fuck out of here." I waved her off.

A while back, before I handled Keyona, my siblings tried to put me in a damn mental ward. I thought we were all just going to lunch. When we pulled up in front of the crazy house, they had me fucked up.

"Mannn, we was just playing with your sensitive ass. Real shit bro, I'm happy you're doing a lot better. You look a lot better too. All daddyish and shit. Owee-wee!" she hyped me up, laughing the whole time. I waved her off, joining her in hysterics.

"Man, gon' head with your silly ass. If you don't have any more questions, I have somewhere to be."

"Let me find out you have to date. I'm telling Rizz!" she joked.

"Oh, she knows," I revealed without saying too much.

"Mhm, okay. I'm going to leave this here in case you change your mind about John." She slid the folder across my desk before turning to leave. I caught it before it flew off my desk.

"It's Sean, nigga!" I yelled at her back.

Liz didn't respond. She threw up a peace sign and kept going. Shaking my head, I stuffed the folder in my computer bag and left too.

Pulling into the driveway of my new house, I noticed Rizz's whip already sitting there. *Oh boy*, I took a deep breath, preparing for whatever was wrong. I knew she had a meeting with her board of directors today. Rizz was up for partner at her firm. I was a thousand percent sure she'd get it.

Entering the house, I found her chilling on the couch with her legs stretched out on the coffee table. I didn't even get mad. This was how she did when she came over. Shit, I wouldn't hesitate to do it at her crib.

"Hey, Rizz." I nodded to her. She was busy staring

down at her thick thighs in the black leggings she wore. As I got closer, I looked for what she could've been so focused on.

I waved my hand in front of her face. "Rizz? You good?"

She shook her no, deeply sniffling. "No," her voice cracked, and she looked up at me.

My heart skipped a beat hearing the pain behind her voice and tears in her eyes. Something told me that nigga, Sean, had every bit to do with this.

"What happened?" I asked anyway. I didn't want to go assuming, shoving my foot in my mouth.

"Sean broke up with me...that's not why I'm crying, though. I was going to break up with his weak ass anyway." She seethed, angry tears and a mean expression twisting her face.

My eyebrows furrowed in confusion. "Then what's up?"

"That muthafucka was using me this whole time!" she screamed, kicking the edge of the coffee table. She looked up me to say something about the table. I threw my hands up in defense.

I couldn't say shit if I wanted to. She bought the shit for me as a 'housewarming' gift. In fact, you might as well say everything in the house was a gift from her. She'd decorated, so she could break whatever she pleased.

I wouldn't front like I wasn't happy to hear that they broke up because...I was happy as a stripper when a baller came and made it rain. I wasn't going to front like I wasn't upset either. "How the fuck?"

"He stole all my notes for my presentation. Like, everything! I couldn't even do the presentation for partner because he stole it. Now, this ass eating prick is my boss!"

"Well…" Honestly, I didn't know what to say. I knew I didn't like that nigga. Here I was feeling bad about having him investigated, and my gut was right.

"Go ahead and say, 'I told you so'." She rolled her eyes, sitting up straight.

"I told you so," I shrugged.

"Rell!" she shrieked, jumping up and slapping me in the upper arm.

"*Rizz!*" I copied her, minus the hitting.

She narrowed her eyes at me. Shit, I wasn't moved. "Where the food at?" I headed to the kitchen with her on my heels.

"Didn't you order it on the way over?"

"Nigga, no. You said you were bringing Chinese." I grabbed us both a beer out the fridge. Rizz was the only female I knew that drank beer. All the other ones claimed it was nasty. They preferred wine, which was gross to me. Shit tasted like raw meat.

"Now, you should know me better than that."

"You right. Let me go shower and get settled in. You order the food while I do that." I called over my shoulder.

Pop!

"Okay, I got you boo." She threw at my back. I didn't bother turning around. She just popped open a bottle of wine. This was going to be a long night.

"And then, he said I wasn't on *his level*. What kind of shit is that?!" Rizz continued to vent to me about her day after we ate. We were chilling on the couch now. "Do you know how many nights I stayed up preparing for my presentation?!"

"Yes, I do know. We stayed up on the phone three nights in a row, remember?" I reminded her. She nodded, taking a sip of her third glass of wine. "You want to slow down on the wine, alkie?"

"Whatever!" she waved me off, throwing the wine back and pouring herself another glass. I didn't know why I never noticed before, but my best friend was a low-key wino.

"Don't you think you've had enough for one night?"

Slurping the wine down, she shook her head no. She was about to pour herself another drink. This time, I took the bottle away from her. I couldn't stand to watch her make herself sick because Sean decided he wasn't man enough to hold her down.

I knew there was something I didn't trust about him. This was proof right here. He was after her job this whole time.

"Relly! Just one more glass." Rizz slurred, getting up from the couch just to fall back in her seat.

"Nope. You need to lie down and rest yourself," I told her, coming back into the living room. I'd taken our plates and glasses into the kitchen. Taking a seat on the couch, Rizz laid back and rested her head in my lap.

For a moment, we sat there in silence. Glancing down at her, I saw that her eyes were closed. "You sleep?"

"Mn-mn." She shook her head no, licking her lips. I took a moment to just stare at her face while her eyes were still closed.

Man, Rizz was so beautiful to me. From her big, slanted brown eyes, thick and soft lips, to her cute little, pointed nose. She smiled, showing her pretty teeth.

"Stop staring at me, creeper." She giggled. Even in her tipsy state, she was beautiful.

"How you know I'm staring at you?"

"I can see you," she noted in a matter-of-fact tone.

"Nigga, your eyes are closed, though," I pointed out in a know-it-all tone.

She giggled at first, "That doesn't mean that I can't see you, Relly."

"What's that supposed to mean? You see me when you close your eyes or something?"

She nodded, never opening her eyes. "Yes. That's exactly what I mean, Israel. I can't help but to see only you. When I close my eyes, I see us together. While it feels right, it scares me…"

"Why does it scare you?" I wanted to know.

"I've always harbored more than friend feelings for you. Yet, we remain friends…*best friends*. We get by just fine that way. I want to be more, but I also don't want to lose my best friend." she revealed her feelings. She may've been tipsy, yet I knew she meant what she was saying.

Honestly, I felt the same way. I didn't want to ruin our friendship either. I did want to be in a relationship with her, though. She was right. What if we didn't make it?

"Well then, we won't cross that line ever again…" It hurt to say those words, but it is what it is.

"What you mean?" Her eyes popped opened.

"I mean what I said. If us crossing that line scares you, we don't need to do it."

She sat up and turned around on the couch. "How do you feel?"

"You already know how I feel, Rizz. Yes, I'm just as scared as you. Do I want to see where this could go? Yes.

Not if you're not sure or don't want to do it." I gave her the truth.

"I feel you," she nodded, blankly staring ahead. I couldn't read her.

"What's wrong?"

Shaking her head, she pressed her lips together. "Nothing, umm…I better get going. I have a long day at work tomorrow."

Even though I knew she wasn't lying about having work in the morning, there was something else. Rizz knew she could crash in one of the guest bedrooms. She never had a problem before.

"Umm…" I wanted to say more. I wanted to ask a billion questions. I also didn't want to start an argument or some shit. "Okay, I'll see you out."

She grabbed her purse and heels from the floor and headed to the door. I opened the door for her. Before she walked out the house, we embraced in a comforting hug. I kissed her cheek and she proceeded out.

CHAPTER 15

KORI

You ever been in a room full of people physically, but mentally you're somewhere else? That was me right now. Physically, I was in the room with my girls. Mentally, I was with Lah on some beach fucking his brains out.

It'd been a little over three months and we still hadn't had sex yet. While it was refreshing, it was torture, especially because we were under each other a lot. If it wasn't at work, it was at one of our houses.

While these three months had been torture due to no sex, it also brought us closer. I'd learned so much about Islah, and vice versa. It was also crazy how many similarities we had.

Finding out that we were both foodies was the best thing. That was something I'd hid from him at first. I was afraid to show him that side of me because I didn't want to be judged. Little did I know, he was one too. It came out on our first real date.

We were out to eat at this Mexican grill one day. He caught me licking and biting my bottom lip while bucking my eyes over my food. I didn't know he noticed me until he called me out. I tried to cover it up with an excuse. He wasn't buying it, though. He basically told me that if I wanted this thing to work, I had to be as real as he was being with me.

I ended up telling him and this nigga laughed at me. I was embarrassed. I wanted to get up and run somewhere and hide. He must've saw the look on my face because he shut his ass up. He then explained that he felt the same way about food. He told me there was nothing wrong with loving food. He didn't judge me because he was the same way. Even if he wasn't, he wouldn't judge me.

That day, we ordered pretty much everything on the menu, including peach and pomegranate margaritas. We ate and drank until we were full. After, he took me home. We ended up at the park, walking hand in hand, talking and laughing about everything under the sun.

Lah might've been an asshole at times. That was just a shield he used to protect his feelings. What I didn't understand was that he had two parents that were in love and had been that way since before he was born. Why did he have such a hard time falling in love?

He explained that he believed in it. He just hadn't found the right one yet. He did admit that I was the first woman to hold his attention in forever. I thought it was sweet, but I didn't let it go to my head.

"Hellooo…earth to Kori Casique," Liz waved her hands in my face, sitting next to me. We were getting pedicures at *Pretty Lady*. Paris and Yanna had gotten theirs already and moved on to their nails. Liz and I did that part, so we were getting our feet done now.

"Bryant. Kori Bryant." I corrected her.

"Yeah, aight. You know you marrying my brother."

I waved her off. "Y'all swear."

Peeking over in Paris and Yanna's direction, I noticed my cousin wore a solemn expression. I frowned, figuring it was because of her and Sean's break up. I hated that he did my cousin like that. Paris didn't deserve that shit at all. She was too good of a woman. Every night, I prayed that she'd come to her senses and just give Rell a chance. I could tell she wanted to be more than just friends with him.

"How you doing, Paris boo?" I called out to her. Her head turned in my direction and she wore a slight smile.

"I'm good, boo. How are you?"

"I'm good." I gushed, thinking about my baby Islah. "This isn't about me, though. This is about you. How are you really doing?"

Knowing her, she was putting on a smile to keep us from being worried about her. It'd always been like this. Paris constantly felt the need to be the strong/tough one.

"I know you ain't still mad over that gay nigga, John." Liz blurted, causing Paris to turn her nose up.

"Hell no! Fuck him. I don't think he's gay, though." Even when she was mad at the nigga, she defended him. We felt like Sean had a little sugar in his tank. Paris swore up and down he didn't. I mean, what kind of man would give up a woman fine as my cousin? He had to be stupid, crazy, or gay. Sean was too smart and sane, so gay he was. Whatever, time would tell.

"I still can't believe he did you like that, boo." Yanna shook her head.

"It's whatever. I'm over it. I knew it wasn't going to work anyway." Paris slumped her shoulders.

"You're damn right. Rell wasn't having it." Liz laughed, joking to make light of the situation. That didn't seem to do anything but make Paris irritated.

"Nah, he don't care what I do. He just wants me happy." That was good news, yet she was spitting it out like it was leaving a bad taste.

"That's a good thing, isn't it?" I asked.

"Yeah, I guess…"

"This is what you wanted, sis. You don't seem happy that he's not breathing down your neck anymore." Yanna pointed out. I noticed it too. This is what I meant. Paris wanted that man, and bad.

"It's not that. I just…I don't know anymore." She shook her head.

"What?" we were all glued in. The nail tech handling her was even in the mix.

"It's just…Rell used to care more than he's been portraying. It's like he…" She bit her bottom lip, thinking of the right thing to say.

"Gave up on you?" I tried to help her out.

"*Us*…" her voice cracked. "I mean, does he not care about me anymore?"

Liz loudly exasperated. "You know he does. Don't get him caring about you and his feelings for you mixed up, sis."

"Liz is right, Rizz. Rell cares about you. He's just letting up on you. You, of all people, should know that you can't beat a dead horse." Yanna added her knowledge.

"Look, if you have feelings for him, you need to tell him before somebody else snatches him up." I wasn't trying to come across harsh, but it needed to be said.

There was no need in ignoring the big ass elephant in

the room. Paris wanted Rell. She was mad because he didn't seem to still have the feelings he once did. I'm sure there was a perfectly logical explanation.

"Well damn, Lah Jr." Liz laughed out loud. I waved her off with a smirk.

"No, she's right. I need to tell Rell how I feel." Rizz nodded her head in agreeance with me. I offered her a reassuring smile.

"Finally, shit, damn! I thought this day would never come." Liz threw her hands up like she was praising God. I shook my head at her silly ass.

My Baby: Where you at? I miss you.

I smiled like a fool at Lah's text. My heart skipped a beat, and I began to feel all tingly on the inside.

Me: I'm at the salon getting my nails and feet done. I miss you too.

My Baby: Good! Baby, I didn't want to say nothing, but them shits was starting to look bad.

Me: LOL! Fuck you, Islah!

My Baby: Shit, when? Cause a nigga tired of using lotion.

Me: Oml, bye nasty. Lol.

My Baby: Aight, beautiful. Hurry up and come home to me.

Me: Your place or mine?

My Baby: What you think?

I thought about it before texting back. We were at my place more than anything. He now had a key, so he didn't have to break in anymore. Lah just made himself right at home.

Me: You might as well just move in, lbs.

My Baby: Shit, I thought I did.

I was going to text him back until Liz' nosey ass got all

up in my texts, peeking at my phone. "Aww! Y'all so fucking cute, fam! Everybody all in love. *Yasss!*"

Shoving her away, I put my phone up. "Bye, nosey!"

"What's going on with you and Shanah, by the way?" I decided to turn the tables and get in her business. Liz was always rooting for her brother's relationships. Yet, none of them seemed to do the same for her. I couldn't say if it was because she was the youngest, or if it was because she was struggling with her sexuality.

The bright smile on her face faded. "We good…"

"Why do I get the feeling y'all not good?" I asked her with raised eyebrows.

She slumped her shoulders. "I don't know. You're reading too much into things."

"Y'all are still seeing each other? Right?" Yanna caught on to the convo. The tech dealing with her had just finished painting her nails. She was blowing the polish on them now.

"Wrong. She ended things. She said we were moving too fast, she needed time to think or whatever…" Liz dryly replied, waving the conversation off.

"Well, Lizzy…" Paris swiveled around in her chair, now blowing on her nails. "Y'all did move kind of fast. You were claiming ol' girl like the first day. I don't know if you were just playing or not. I would've quit your fatal ass too."

Liz cut her eyes. "Sheesh, that makes me feel so much better."

Paris shrugged, blowing on her nails. "I call it like I see it."

"Oh, yeah? Like you seen Rell had feelings, yet you constantly shrugged them off?" Liz countered. Rizz stopped blowing her nails and squinted her eyes. I could see this turning into a full-blown argument.

Before Paris could fix her lips to speak, I spoke up. "Hey, hey now. We're all friends here. Liz, I'm sorry you're upset about Shanah. Rizz is right, though. Y'all moved kind of fast."

"Thank you—" Paris was about say before I quickly interrupted her.

"Liz is right, Paris. You've been running from that man too long. You sit here wondering why he's acting different. You can only be shrugged off so many times until you give up."

She wanted to say something, yet nothing was coming out her mouth. She was moving her lips open, then closing them. I turned to Liz and she had almost the same reaction. Yanna was looking at me with a smirk.

"Whatever Lah did to you, I like it." She laughed out loud. "I hate to break up the party ladies, but I have to get back to work."

"Have a good day, boo!" I cheered in excitement.

My Baby: Where you at? It's been an hour.

Side-eyeing the text I got from Lah, I laughed out loud.

Me: You a lie. It's barely been fifteen minutes. I'm glad to know you miss me, though.

"I'm going to head out too. I have a few things to handle at the office." Paris tossed her bag over her shoulder and threw up a peace sign before leaving. Liz followed suit, not saying a word though.

Were they mad or nah? I shrugged my shoulders, not caring. They both knew I was right. *Oh well, they'll get over it.*

Walking into the house, I was greeted by a trail of red rose petals and white candles, leading into the living room. Following the trail, Joe x "I Want to Know" caressed my eardrums. I also smelled a savory aroma coming from the kitchen. The smell reminded me of my mother's cooking, yet I knew it wasn't her who had set all of this up. This had Islah Perez Casique written all over it.

"Baby?" I called out to him, stopping in the middle of the living room. I spotted a folded-up note resting on the table.

Stop asking questions (yes you are) and follow the trail. P.S.: I know you smell what I'm cooking, but don't go into the kitchen first.

Ugh, I swear he was irky. He was right, though. I wanted to go into the kitchen and see what smelled so good. Besides making sandwiches and a quick breakfast, he'd never cooked for me.

Going against my stomach's judgment, I continued to follow the trail of roses and candles. I was led to the bathroom in the bedroom. On the counter was another note.

Take off your clothes and step into the tub.

I did exactly what I was told and took my clothes off. I bet Lah was having himself a good laugh wherever he was. The notes were comical. He knew I didn't like being told what to do. I also didn't follow instructions well. He claimed it was one of the many things he loved about me. We were alike in that way. This nigga took shit from no one.

Sitting in the tub felt so good, so relaxing. I needed this after a long week of work. Lately, I'd been helping Lah get things in order with the family's businesses. At first, it started off as me doing most of the work. That is, until I told him my job description.

I wasn't there to do much of anything, except give my advice. Since he was my man, I wasn't going to leave him hanging, so I threw in a helping hand. Once we got that out the way, he was on it.

Pops had come by a few times to check up on him. Each time, he nodded his head in approval. I could tell that it made Lah feel good to have his father's approval. Watching him happy and smiling was the highlight of my day.

"*My whole life has changed since you came in...*" I sang along as the song changed. I loved this song so much. I always imagined dancing to this song at my wedding. I made jokes with Lah about us getting married all the time. I didn't mean any of it. I was simply enjoying the time we were spending. I didn't know what the future held.

Knock, knock.

My eyes popped open, and Lah was standing in the door entrance. I licked my lips at him. He was wearing nothing but boxers and tube socks. I couldn't help or stop my eyes traveling to his swollen dick print. I bit my bottom lip, taking a deep breath. *Chill, Kori,* I told myself.

"Quit raping me with your eyes, perv," he scoffed with a smirk.

Kissing my teeth, I waved him off. "Whatever, punk. Ain't nobody worried about you."

"Oh yeah?" he swaggered over to the tub and knelt to the floor. He stared me in the eyes. It was so intense, I always had to look away first. The only time I could keep eye contact was when I was pissed with him.

"You miss me?" I broke our silence.

She shook his head. "Nope."

"Lies."

Next, another one of my favorite songs, "Crazy Over You" x Sonta, came on. He winked at me, knowing I got off to this song. I knew it word for word. Listening to it just did something to me.

"*It's a certain way you make me feeeel…I go crazyyyy over youuu booy…*" I couldn't help but sing to him. "*I know I'm on your mind after what happened last night. But I don't want to hit your line even though you are on mine. You so fine, I want your time. Can't hide the way I feel…*"

"*Your legs up on my shoulders. It's time, let's take it slow…*" he sang, switching the words around in his favor. I broke out in a fit of laughter.

"You're so nasty."

"You knew this, though…" He was right. I knew it. "You wash your ass yet?"

I shook my head, laughing. "I swear I can't stand your ass."

"Yeah, yeah, I'm feeling your ass too, ma. You ready to get out?" he stood, holding his hand to me. I took his hand and allowed him to wrap a towel around my body. He pulled me closer, laying a sensual kiss on my lips. I wanted him more now than ever.

"Thank you," I blurted.

"For what?"

I took a step back and spread my arms out. "This. I appreciate it so much. I know what you're going to say… *don't ruin the moment with this corny shit,*" I mimicked his ass.

"Shut up. You don't know me, nigga." He grabbed me

around the waist, kissing me some more. I allowed his tongue to explore my mouth.

"Mmm." A moan broke free from deep within me.

"You know I'm getting some tonight." he stated, grabbing my ass and picking me up.

"It's your night. I'm following if you're leading."

He led me back downstairs to the dining room table. My eyes lit up at the sight before me. "You made me surf n' turf!"

"Correction. I made *us* surf n' turf." He pulled the chair out for me.

"There's only one plate, though." I was greedy, so I knew he didn't think I was sharing a plate.

"Exactly. We're eating off the same plate. Don't worry. I'm going to feed your greedy ass." He laughed.

After eating, he led me back upstairs to the bedroom. He had me in daze, floating on an imaginary cloud. He was being so gentle and loving with me.

This was a side of him I rarely saw. He was only like this during heart to hearts. Otherwise, he was an asshole 25/8. Me being under him all the time, his attitude was wearing off on me.

"Mmm, this feels so good, baby…" I cooed as he rubbed my body down with the same natural oils, I used on him a few of weeks ago. I saw how stressed out he was and wanted to do something special that didn't involve sex. That night, I set his room up like I was trying to get something started. I had his ass fooled, though.

"You deserve it, mami."

"Can I do you after you do me?" I asked in complete relaxation.

"Nah, this all for you. It's all about you tonight. Let your man cater to you. You always got me covered."

A big smile graced my face, hearing those words leave his mouth. "Okay."

"Thank you," he replied.

"For what?"

"Everything." He flipped me over to lie on my back. He poured the oil on my chest, breasts, and stomach. I moaned deeply as he rubbed it in.

"You put up with my attitude with a smile. You always here when a nigga needs you. You show and teach me things I never knew shit about. You make me a better man, Kori. That's real shit."

"Aww, baby…*well…*" I bashfully cheesed. He was making me feel super vulnerable.

"I love you," he blurted next.

My eyes popped open and I sat up on the bed. He was looking me dead in the eyes. I was trying to convince myself I didn't hear him right. Maybe I was just caught up in the moment and was just hearing shit.

"I said I love you." he said it again.

I grabbed his face, pulling him in for a kiss. "I love you too! You don't know how long I waited to hear you say that."

The truth is, I'd already fallen in love with him. I just didn't know when the right time would be. As I said, he was an asshole. I always imagined me saying it and his rude ass shooting it down.

"Not as long as I've wanted to do this…" He kissed my lips, then laid me back. I was confused by what he was saying.

"Huh? What are you talking—"

The rest of my words got lost somewhere in the middle of my heart when I felt my legs shuffle over his shoulders and his thick tongue parted my southern lips. *Oh God, is this happening?* I could've laid there and took the good tongue lashing he was giving me. Believe me, I wanted to, BUT I couldn't help myself.

I pushed his head away and scooted as far as the bed would allow before I hit the wall. Lah was glaring at me like I'd stolen his sandwich last week, which I did.

"You said you wouldn't eat pussy unless it was your wife!" I didn't mean to scream, but I couldn't help myself.

He palmed his face and shook his head. "I know what I said, woman."

"Okay, then what the hell are you doing?"

"Lower your voice."

"What are you doing?" I squeaked out.

Blowing out a breath of frustration, he threw his hands up and turned to go in the bathroom. "You know, most women would just take the head and be satisfied. But nooo, not you."

I heard the water running and got off the bed. Oh Lord, I had ruined the moment. I got off the bed to go comfort him in the bathroom. "Baby, I'm sorry. I didn't mean to make you—"

Again, my words were stuck in my chest. My air supply was damn near punched out my lungs. Oh God, Oh God, Oh God!

Lah was on one knee, holding a box open with a diamond ring inside. I was in so much shock, I could've pissed on myself right now. "I was trying to do this like on the movies. I surprise you with some romantic shit, we make love, I do something I said I'd never do. Then, you wake up with the ring on your finger."

"I…"

"Look baby, I know this is super soon. I'm still trying to wrap my mind around the shit. I was talking to Ma and Pops about it for two weeks. They kept telling me to go for it. Finally, I grew the courage to ask you…" He got choked up.

I turned the water off and got on my knees in front of him. "Baby…"

"Please, ma. Let me get this out." He grabbed my face and kissed me. I nodded, tears surfacing at the rims of my eyes. I didn't realize they were there until one slipped out.

"You do cry!" He smiled hard. I laughed, confused.

"The hell? Of course, I do! Look at what you're doing right now."

"Okay, serious moment…Kori," he stopped and laughed harder. "Y'all, stop filming. We got her. She cries."

He was laughing, but I wasn't anymore. I was becoming annoyed.

"What the—"

"I'm just playing, baby. Will you marry me?" He returned to his original serious state.

"No!" I mugged him and stood up.

His face dropped in disbelief. I cracked a smile. "Just kidding! Of course, I'll marry you baby—"

"Nope." He shook his head and stood up. "I don't want to marry you no more. You ruined it."

I snatched the ring out his hand and slipped it on my finger. "Shut up. You're marrying my ass. You ain't about to have my ass crying for no reason!"

"I love you! I swear I do." He pulled me close.

"I love you too, ugly." I was being completely serious.

"You scared?"

I nodded, "Shitless."

"Me too," he admitted with a deep breath.

"At least we're scared together."

"At least…" He shrugged.

"What are you thinking about?" I could tell he was thinking something.

"I'm thinking about doing something else crazy." He smiled evilly at me.

I squinted my eyes at him. Call it fate or whatever, but a part of me knew what it was. "Like?"

"Let's go get married…right now." He was saying it but wanted my nod of approval.

"Your ass just wants some head!"

"You're damn right!" he chuckled. I joined him in laughter. "Real shit, I just want you to share my last name."

The real tears finally fell. I nodded. "Let's do it."

CHAPTER 16

LAH

The next day...
Virgin Islands (British)

Yup. A nigga went ahead and proposed. The shit seemed out of pocket crazy. Well, I was crazy for the woman I wanted to carry my last name. I didn't want to wait for her to have it either.

Right now, Kori was following my lead, just winging it. The fact that it was completely out of her comfort zone and she was doing it for me said enough. I was wifing this woman. Any female that rode with her man with no questions, trusted him with everything, and backed him up? It's a wife fam.

I tried to plan out the perfect proposal, set her up with something special. Shit didn't work in my favor, though. For one, Kori asked way too many questions. I almost didn't propose after she pushed my head away when I was trying to eat her pussy. It was a part of my surprise proposal. Believe me, I was nervous as shit. Low key, I was happy she stopped me. It gave me enough time to get my nerves together and question if I was really about to do this.

Her pushing my head away also proved something to me. She wasn't going to let me do something I vowed not to do. To me, that was everything. She showed me right there that she had my best interest at heart.

Knock. Knock.

"You ready?" Pops poked his head into the hotel room, asking. I did a once over of myself in the mirror. I had on an all-white cotton linen suit and these brown Jesus sandals. Hey, it wasn't my choice. Kori wanted to come here and tie the knot, looking like a damn hippie. I figured what we were doing was crazy enough. Why not go all hippy dippy?

"Uh, yeah. I'm ready." I breathed a sigh of relief.

"You sure? This is a huge step. Marriage isn't something to play with, son." he lectured. I shook my head, putting my hand on his shoulder.

"I get that, Pops. I know, really. This is the woman that I love, and I want to marry. I don't want to wait to tie the knot either."

He put his head down and lightly chuckled. "When you came to me for advice two weeks ago, I knew you would propose. Now, here we are and you're about to get married. Excuse me if I'm a little thrown off, son."

"I know you're looking out for my best interest. Kori does it for me, Pops. She's the one I want to spend the rest of my life with. I love her, and the feeling is mutual."

"I hear you, son. I just want you to be sure about what you're doing."

I nodded my head, paying attention in the mirror. "Let

me ask you something, Pops…how long did it take you to know that Ma was the one for you?"

His face dropped into a smile. He pointed at me, cheesing and shaking his head. "You sneaky little nigga. I see what you did there."

"Aha!" I pointed back at him, laughing.

My pops fell in love with Ma the moment he laid eyes on her. He knew, in that moment, she was going to be his wife. God favored him enough to make Ma feel the same way. Ma wasn't one of those females who just let a nigga like Pops pursue her. She used to always joke about she should've married a lawyer, doctor, or some shit. Instead, she ended up with a street nigga.

In some ways, Kori reminded me of my Ma. If you looked and listened to her, you'd assume she was married to some square ass nigga. Kori was quiet, sophisticated, and didn't know the first thing about how to shoot a gun. That was Ma when she met Pops. She was green, pure, yet ready for anything. That was Kori, through and through.

I actually liked that about her, though. I never imagined myself marrying a woman like her—*getting married at all*. My heart was tight, stomach in knots. I was taking deep breaths and talking to myself in my head.

"Lah!" Pops blurted out, snapping me from my thoughts. Shaking my head, I pulled my attention toward him. "You good?"

"Yeah." I nodded.

"Okay, I'm going to go find your mother and make sure she's good."

Before he walked, I called out to him. "You and Ma good, right?"

"Yeah. We're good." he answered, making no eye

contact. He was lying. I couldn't focus on that too much right now. I was going to get into that later, though.

After getting myself together, I was headed downstairs to share a drink with Pops, Isi, and Rell.

"Will you guys stop asking me that already? Sheesh! I love—*I'm in love with Islah*, and I want to marry him." I heard Kori say. The way our rooms were set up, all I had to do was open the door joining the rooms.

Next, I heard Rizz's voice. "Okay, and we get that. We're just trying to make sure this is what you really want. I mean, Aunt Viv isn't even here."

"It is what I really want. Mama didn't want to come. She has a phobia of flying. Now, can you spend more time helping me get ready?"

"I'm just saying. Y'all moving a little fast—"

"At least I know what I want!"

The room was silent until Rizz asked, "What's that supposed to mean?"

"Oh, come on, Rizz! You know what I mean. You've been feeling it for Rell since forever. You're in love with that man, yet you won't be honest with him. Look, I'm in love with Islah. It didn't take me twenty damn years to figure it out either. Keep on and you're going to lose out on Rell."

I was smiling hard as fuck right now. I didn't know what I was about to hear. I was happy to know that my baby was sure. Just hearing those words made me feel so much better. Yup, it's a wife.

We were now chilling on the beach, enjoying each other, watching the sunset on the waves and smoking a blunt. The fam was roaming the island, enjoying themselves as well. It felt good to be away from the States and have everybody here with us. Even though it wasn't planned, this trip was much needed for our family.

"Can you believe we just did that?" Kori giddily exclaimed. I was full of the same energy as her, just cool about it.

"I believe it, babe. You happy?"

She placed her hands around my face, straddling my lap. "I'm so happy, baby."

"Good...that's all that matters to me." Briefly, I smiled at her.

"What's wrong? You're not happy, baby?"

"No, I'm happy. I just want to make sure that you're always happy. I know I can be an asshole at times, but real shit ma, I care more about your happiness than my own." I spoke from the heart, something I was becoming accustomed to since being with Kori.

She loved to have heart to hearts. At first, I got tired of them. I wasn't a touchy-feely ass nigga. Seeing that they made her feel good, I did it for her. Now, I was doing them on my own. Man, this woman had infected me.

"Aww, you're being so sweet. Who knew you had it in you?" she sarcastically spat in a laugh.

Shaking my head, I laughed too. "Whatever, nigga. For you, I will be anything."

"*For you, I will!*" she sang off-key.

"Aye, what I tell you about making my ears bleed? Can you pass the blunt back? Damn, just smoking up all my shit." I took the blunt back. "I thought you never smoked before."

Believe it or not, this was her first time. My baby was laying between my legs, high as a damn kite. She was giggling like crazy. Tears kept rushing her eyes, but she'd swiped them away.

"I haven't, and I see why now." she giggled, rolling in the sand.

"Let's go back inside now, babe." I helped her up. She let my hand go once she up. She was walking toward the waves with her arms open. She got to the imaginary line where the waves stop and stood there. I watched my beautiful wife with a smile. Kori was so happy and free, which made me happy and free. Man, if this was what love felt like, I didn't want it to go away.

"Baby! Let's go swimming!" She began to rush into the waves. I went after her little crazy high ass.

"Hell no, ma. See, it's time for you to go back in. You had too much weed." I caught up to her, out of breath.

"Come, babe," she whined, feeling me up. She stuck her hands in my pants, stroking my dick. "Remember when I told you this would be all mine?" she slurred.

"Mhm, and you were right," I admitted.

"I know." She winked. Before I knew it, she was in a squatting position, snatching my dick out my pants.

"Whoa, baby w—" I tried to stop her, but she shut my ass up, swallowing my shit whole. Gotdamn! "Baby...this, isn't right," I managed to cry out like a bitch. It'd been so long since I'd had sex or my dick sucked, I couldn't help but to stand there and enjoy it.

"You like that, daddy?" She came up for air, spitting on the head.

"Shiiit, ma. What the fuck are you doing? We in the middle—"

Again, she shut me up with her stupid ass head. I was enjoying this shit, but I also was scared. We were damn near in the middle of the ocean! Not really, but from my perspective, we were close.

Kori came back up, kissing me in the mouth. She was still stroking me up. "Come on baby, relax and enjoy this." She jumped on me.

"Babe, I want to, but shit…" I moaned as she continued to stroke my dick with her little hands. "We, we in the middle of the water."

"We are not!" she giggled. "Plus, this is something I always wanted to do. Who better than to do it with than my husband?"

"What? Get fucked in the ocean?"

"Mhm." She poked her bottom lip out, giving me the puppy dog eyes.

"Don't do that shit to me right now, baby." I shook my head.

"Don't you want this pussy, daddy?" She lifted up, placing her hand between her legs. I didn't know what she was doing until I felt her warm opening thrusting on my manhood.

"Shit, yees!" I hollered. "But baby, what if we die?"

She stared in my eyes, smirking like a maniac. "Til' death do us part, baby."

Damn. I had to go and marry a crazy woman. Kori was it for me though. I wasn't letting her little ass go.

CHAPTER 17

YANNA

Two weeks later…

"Have I told you I love you today?" Isi asked me, kissing the back of my hand as we entered the community center. I smiled up at him, stopping to pull his lips against mine.

"Yes, but I love hearing it. I love you more." We'd just come back from having lunch after seeing Dr. Herguth.

Rell recommended her to us. He spoke so highly of her that we had to give her a try. We'd made it very clear that we were happily in love and our marriage was fine. We just wanted to come and air our feelings about the miscarriage. So far, it was working out well.

On top of seeing her, we kept prayer equivalent. We prayed before we went to sleep, when we woke up, and before we left each other at any given time of the day. Prayer was pulling us closer. I didn't think we could get any closer. I was wrong.

I never, until now, realized how much Isi and I were

apart. I was either out with the girls or at the mansion with Ma and Mama. He was always at work. That had all changed. We were doing more together now than ever.

It's crazy how you can think your marriage is fine and it's not as fine as you thought. I'm just happy we caught it before it got serious. Dr. Herguth found it cute and funny how easily we got along. She said she never met a couple so perfect for each other.

"Ms. Yanna! Look what I drew for you!" Ayanna ran over to us. She wore a huge smile. Every time I saw her, she was smiling so bright. It made my day.

When I met her, she was on the steps crying and didn't know where or what was going to happen to her. Since then, Sade had been keeping her at her house. She was searching the system for a good home for her. I was helping when I had the time.

All the ones we came across were either full or had bad reports. Ayanna had won over both our hearts. We didn't want to see anything bad happen to her. Even though we were both compromising our careers, we kept looking. Something had to give. Her mother hadn't even showed back up to come get her. From what Sade told me, it was a lost cause. Since this wasn't her first time doing this, there was no telling when she'd be coming back. I wish I could find that bitch and give her a piece of my mind.

Every night since then, I'd gone to bed praying for the woman and Ayanna. I prayed Ayanna found a loving home, and that her mother got serious help. It didn't seem like she was missing her mother. However, I knew better. She was just good at hiding her emotions.

"Aww! This is beautiful, Yanna!" I beamed, calling her by her nickname. I thought it was so cute how we had the same nickname. "Baby, look. We have a little artist on our hands."

"That's very nice, Lil' Yanna," he called her by the nickname he'd come up for her. I liked it. I was Big Yanna and she was Lil' Yanna. I watched the beam in my husband's eyes and couldn't help but smile.

Since I introduced him to Lil' Yanna, he was doing his best to help me and Sade find her a home. He was coming up to the center to visit the kids too. Shit, he was here so much, he might as well have filled out an application. Watching him interact with the kids made me happy.

At first, it took a little minute to get used to. Even though we were working through it, I still had I little doubt in the back of my mind. It was telling me that I'd never be able to give my husband a child. That's when I prayed the hardest.

We'd stopped trying for a kid too. Dr. Herguth advised we stop trying. The more we try, the more disappointed we'd be if we didn't get pregnant. She was right. That's how it was when we were trying. Trying also took the fun out of sex.

Knock. Knock.

"Oop," I giggled when our make-out session in my office was interrupted.

"Come in," we answered in unison. The door opened and Sade stepped into the office.

"I hope I'm not interrupting anything." She giggled.

"Girl no, you're good." I smiled, waving her off. "Have a seat. What's up?" It felt good to say that. I was loving that I took a step out on faith to finally follow my dreams.

Isi was happy too. I could see it in his eyes every time he showed up to pick me up and dropped me off at work.

He didn't have to, but he loved it. He'd drop me off at the center and then head to the office.

"Well, that's my cue. I'll see you later, baby." He pecked my lips. "See you, sis."

"Umm, I need to talk to the both of you, bro." Sade called out to him before he could touch the door handle. Isi backpedaled and came to stand next to me.

"What's up?" he inquired. She had both our attention.

"It's about Lil' Yanna…" She sighed, shaking her head. She hadn't told us what it was, but I felt my stomach churning and heart beating faster.

"What is it, sis?" Isi beat me to the question, panic filling his voice like it was my loins.

"I can't find a decent home for her. Everything is either full or just…fucked up. I reached out to her other relatives that showed up in the system. They don't want her. She had a grandmother she stayed with at one point, but she's deceased. I don't—"

"*We'll take her!*" Isi and I both blurted out. We stared at each other with wide eyes. I wasn't expecting him to say that. It was obvious he wasn't expecting me to say it either. Sade's eyes widened as well.

"I wasn't insisting on you guys taking…*are y'all sure about this?*" she asked in shock. I was paralyzed with it myself. A million and one things were running through my mind. I was questioning a lot. One thing sure, though. I wanted Lil' Yanna to come stay with us. I just didn't know Isi felt the same.

"Can you give us a minute, sis?"

Sade shook her head rapidly, getting up. She almost fell, stumbling to get up. "Yeah, let me know."

"Baby?" Isi rubbed my back after the door shut. I looked up at him with a blank expression.

"You want to take Lil' Yanna in?" I found the words I wanted to ask. He nodded.

"It's obvious you do too. How long you been feeling this way?" He pulled me out of my seat, trading places and placing me on his lap.

"Honestly?" I studied his beautiful dark brown orbs. He raised his eyebrows.

"No doubt."

"Since I found her sitting on the stairs. How long have you wanted to take her in?" I countered.

He took a deep breath. "Honestly?"

I nodded. "Always."

"Since you told me about her. I know it sounds crazy, but I did. Seeing you cry about her I had this feeling. Like, a 'we should adopt her' feeling. I know that sounds off…" He shook his head with a perplexed look on his face.

"No, it doesn't sound crazy to me at all. When were you going to tell me how you felt?"

"I was going to say something after I met her in person. It slipped my mind after Sade thought she found a couple the first time. I was going to tell you, baby, I swear—"

I cut him off. "I know you were, babe. I was going to tell you too. I was just afraid you wouldn't be for it." I revealed with my head down.

He placed his hand under my chin and lifted it. "I'm with it, baby."

I couldn't fight back the tears escaping my eyes. I was overwhelmed with excitement and nervousness. Excitement because we were giving a child a home. Nervous because WE WERE GIVING A CHILD A HOME! Though I knew it wasn't that hard, I didn't know the first thing about being a mother. Other than my mother, Mama Casique and Ma, that's all I knew. I was definitely going to drive Ma and Mama nuts, asking questions.

"Umm, so…there's something else I want to talk to you about…" He seemed nervous to tell me. He tried to move me out his lap, but I wasn't having it. I was sitting my ass right here in case I had to cut him for whatever he was about to say. I knew that's why he wanted to move me.

"Isiah Perez Casique…" I inhaled, shaking my head with a raised eyebrow. "What did you do?"

"I uhh…signed us up for parenting classes." He quickly said it, but I caught every word.

"You did what?!" I squinted my eyes at him. He flinched in his seat.

"Please baby, don't be mad. I love you, I love you, I love you!" He kissed my lips quickly each time he spoke the three-word sentence. I dropped my hard demeanor with a smile. I stood out of his lap and stretched.

"I'm not mad because…I signed us up to be foster parents!"

"You did what?! Baby, without consulting me first?"

I was on the other side of the desk with the quickness. "Well, you signed us up for parenting classes!"

"Aight, aight, aight." He waved me off. "Come here." He used his index finger to summon me.

"Mnt, mnt." I shook my head, dropping to duck behind the chair in front of my desk. He was cracking up on the other side.

"Baby, if you don't bring yo ass over here…"

"No, Ike, I-I-I, I'm sorry. Don't beat me, daddy." I

whined, imitating Anna Mae in my own little way. He was in hysterics.

"Anna Mae…bring yo ass here, girl. N-now don't make me g-get u-up!"

I laid on the floor, laughing my ass off. This fool was something else. Isi came over and helped me up. "I love your silly ass."

I kissed his lips with passion. "I love your silly too."

"You really want to do this, baby?"

"Yes! I really do. Ayanna deserves good parents. I know we never done this before, but I think together, we got this."

"Okay, then it's settled—"

The door opened, and Sade barged in doing a happy dance. "Yaay!"

Me and Isi burst out laughing like crazy.

"How long you been out there?" I placed my hands on my hips.

"Honestly?" she asked innocently. I narrowed my eyes at her. That right there told me she'd heard our entire conversation.

"Nosey ass!" Isi loudly chuckled. He glanced at his watch. "Oh, I have to get back to the office, babe. Sis… thank you so much. I love you." He hugged her and kissed me.

"Thank you so much, Dey." I hugged her tightly.

"No! Thank y'all!"

"So, what do we have to do?" I was ready to get the ball rolling.

"Well, you've made the first step in getting certified. Usually, the state requires you to be certified before taking the child in, but I pulled some strings. Told them the situation and circumstances. Let them know there was a lovely couple that wanted to take Lil' Yanna in immediately. You being a social worker wasn't left out either. So, they were showing excitement. Of course, they asked the reasonable questions about her mother and other family. Got that covered too. All you and Isi have to do now is finish the classes. Someone is going to come by on Wednesday and do an inspection. Then, everything is set."

"So, Lil' Yanna can move in on Wednesday?" That's all I heard and cared about. The other stuff sounded good and easy enough. Isi and I kept a clean and drug-free home. Any weapon we had were guns, and they were registered.

"Yes, ma'am!" Sade jumped up and down in excitement. I joined her in excitement and praise.

Thank you, Jesus!

CHAPTER 18
RIZZ

C *ome on Rizz. You can do this. Just...tell him how you feel. Knock on the door and say...* Here I was, pacing back and forth like a crackhead waiting for a fix, on Rell's porch. Shit, I might as well had been one. Me being the crackhead and Rell being the drug. Or was it the other way around? He was feeling me just as bad. At least, I think he was. He'd gone from demanding me to marry him to shrugging me off in a matter of months. The shit hurts!

I wasn't trying to be choosey. I just thought he'd be here when I was ready to come to my senses. I knew me and Sean wouldn't last long. He was too weak for my liking. The nigga was an ass kisser. I hated that more than anything.

While I was pissed the way it happened, I was relieved that we were broken up. How did I get played by his weak ass? Unless...it was all an act. My chain of thought was interrupted as I paced left and right.

The door opened and Rell stood there without a shirt

on. He was only wearing pajama pants. My eyes roamed his beautiful and muscular caramel chest. "Rizz, what are you doing out here this late? It's damn near midnight."

"Umm." Suddenly, I was tongue-tied. Like I couldn't think of what exactly to say. This was unlike me. "I...umm."

I never had this problem—ever! Why was it so hard to say how I felt now?

"Here. Come in the house, ma." He held his hand out to me. Reluctantly, I took it and let him lead me in. "I'm going to get you some water."

Come on Rizz. Why are you scared? Just say how you feel! I screamed in my mind.

"Rell?" I called to him.

He stopped walking toward the kitchen and turned around. "Yes?"

Once again, my mind went blank, and I didn't know what to say. "Rizz? You good?"

"No, I'm not good..." I breathed out.

"What's wrong? Here, come sit down."

Fuck it, I thought, rushing him. Grabbing him by the face, I kissed his lips with all the passion I could muster. He was confused, but kissed me back anyway.

"What's that about?" he rubbed his hand over his mouth.

"I love you, Israel," I confessed, staring into his eyes.

"I love you too, Paris. You know that. So, what's up?" He searched my eyes for answers.

I sucked in a deep breath. I wish this could be like in the movies, where the man would pick the woman up after kissing and go make love. But oh nooo. I was dealing with confused ass Rell.

"I love you more than a friend, Rell. I want to be with you." I confessed to him.

"I thought you said you didn't want to take it there. You wanted to keep it as us just being friends? What happened to that?"

I sucked in a deep breath. *Just be honest with him. Tell him your true feelings*, I spoke to myself with my eyes closed.

"Rizz, you drunk?"

Drunk in love. "No...I'm in love. I know I said I didn't want to mess up our friendship. I still don't, but how do we know it'll be messed up? Unless we try?"

"That's a risk you're willing to take?" he questioned with seriousness.

"You're not?"

I watched him shake his head and take a seat on the sofa. "Why the sudden change of heart?" he questioned. I wasn't expecting him to say that. I imagined this moment, him being happy. He was supposed to run to me, pick me up, toss me in the air—shit, something. Not just sit there wondering why I wanted to be with him.

See, I knew he didn't want to be with me. I knew he changed his heart. It was my fault though. Kori, Liz, and Yanna were all right. I waited too long.

"You told me you'd wait for me to want you. I want you, Rell."

"I umm..." He shook his head.

"What? Say something."

"I uhh...I'm sorry, Rizz." He placed his head in his hands. I went over and took a seat next to him.

"Hey, what's wrong with you? Why are you saying sorry?"

"I was selfish. I shouldn't have put that much pressure on you. You don't have to be with me to make me happy. I'm cool with us being best friends. I want you to be happy with who makes you happy."

"I'm happy with you, Rell. I do want to be with you. I'm not saying that to make you happy. I want this. Only if you do, though."

He pulled his head from his palms, staring into my eyes. "You're serious…" It was like he was having an epiphany. I nodded my head with wide eyes.

"Yes, silly. I'm serious. I know I pushed you away before. It was me stuck in denial. I wanted you just as bad, but I…"

"You were scared," he finished my sentence.

"Yes." I nodded.

"You're serious about this? You want to risk our friendship?"

"Well, when you put it like that, no. We're always going to be friends first. Unless you do something that's unforgivable. Which I know you wouldn't do."

"I did when I was with Ken doll…"

I couldn't stifle the tickle in my stomach. "You finally admit that she's a man."

"Whatever. I'm not saying that. I'm just saying…I'm sorry. I mean, I apologized before, but I never really got over it. Talking to Dr. Herguth has helped a lot."

Thank the Lord! "That's good…" I smiled to him.

It might sound bad, but I was happy he'd gone through this. He was a different man now. For a minute, I thought he had a thing for Dr. Herguth. She was all he seemed to talk about. She had this nigga on some Zen shit.

"So, we for real doing this?" he asked like a broken record.

"Yes! For the thousandth time, yes!"

"Okay, well in that case…" He rushed upstairs, leaving me on the couch. I heard him moving around upstairs. He came back downstairs all out of breath.

"What's this?" I took the envelope out his hand, staring in confusion.

He grabbed my hand, getting on one knee. My heart was beating so loud, I'm sure it was audible. I said we could be together, not get married.

Speaking of which, I was happy for Kori and Lah. I was also concerned they'd moved too fast. Kori talked about how happy she was, but marriage? I thought the shit was crazy. Then again, this was Lah we were talking about. His middle name was crazy.

"If we're going to be together, I want to be honest about everything. I don't want shit popping up out the blue, threatening our relationship. A few months back, I had Liz do some research on your boy, Sean. She dug up everything she could, and this is what she found."

"What's in the envelope?" I wasn't surprised or mad about him investigating Sean. I would've been in the beginning. Now, I was happy. Rell always had my back and for that, I loved him more than anything.

He shrugged his shoulders. "I haven't looked. It'd been so long and I accepted you were going to be with Sean…I didn't feel the need to open it."

"Well, let's see what's inside…"

I opened the envelope and dumped the contents on the table. Rell and I flipped everything over. "Oh my God…is that?"

I picked the picture up, looking closer. My stomach churned with a swish of nausea. Rell looked over my shoulder at the picture in my hand. It was pictures of Sean and some man kissing, hugging, and holding hands.

"What the fuck…" He fell back against the couch.

I couldn't breathe as the tears escaped my eyes. I was thirty-eight hot. This nigga really did play me. He'd been gay this entire time.

My stomach was all over the place. Feeling the vomit touch the back of my throat, I ran to the bathroom. Rell was right there holding my hair and caressing my back.

CHAPTER 19
KORI

I was on my way to my car when I thought I spotted Isi. He was sitting inside an old burnt orange Monte Carlo. I had to do a quick double-take. Something about him was different, and it wasn't just his car. I couldn't place it.

I started to walk over and speak. I stopped when a woman with a black scarf failing to cover her face and neck walked over to the driver's side. She bent over, sticking her head in the window. The next thing happening, Isi was rolling the window up around her neck.

I wanted to go over and help, yet I was stuck in place. Quickly, I got into my car and pulled my phone out. I called the only person I felt could help in this situation.

"What's good, beautiful? You on your way home now?" Lah sweetly answered on the first ring. I couldn't get into all that mushy shit right now.

"Baby, I need you now!" I exclaimed into the receiver.

"Shit, I need you too, girl." His mind was in the gutter, as always.

"No, babe. Shut up and listen. I'm at the salon and I see Isi. He's rolling some woman's head up in his car window. I want to go see what's going on, but I'm scared."

"Shit, where are you now?"

"I'm at *Pretty Lady* on the Northside. I'm seeing this shit right now. What do I do, baby?" I panicked into the receiver.

"The fuck? Don't do a damn thing! I'm on my way."

I heard him talking but didn't know what he was saying. I was too busy trying to see what Isi was doing with this woman. Yanna was just inside the shop. How did she not see her husband in a loud ass Monte Carlo in broad daylight?

"Kori! Do you hear me? Don't. Do. A. Damn. Thing!"

"Wait…he's letting her go…" I spoke in a hushed tone, still watching the scene unfold in front of me.

"Kori—"

I shushed Lah up. "Her scarf fell off her face, babe. Shut up for a minute."

She bent over and hastily picked her scarf up. All the air damn near left my body when I saw who she was.

"Kori, you still there?"

"Baby…" I caught my breath. "It's, Kassidy Kyle…"

"As in your boss?" he asked dumbfounded.

"Yes! As in your crazy ass ex, Kas." I revealed to him.

When I say those three months without sex helped, baby, they helped! We honestly and truly got to get to know each other. We were still finding out little things every day. Within a matter of time, Lah and I had become more like best friends that made out occasionally. Now, we were married. I still couldn't believe it.

"What the fuck is he doing with Kas, man?" Lah mumbled to himself, but I heard him. "Baby, is he still around?"

"I thought you didn't want me to do nothing." I smirked, holding the phone against my ear and shoulder.

I was reaching over, digging in the glove compartment for pen and paper. While he talked, I jotted the make of the car and the license plate number down. I even went ahead and wrote Isi's description down.

This shit was low-key fun. I was starting to feel like maybe I chose the wrong career. I could do this PI shit any day. It was a good thing I had tinted windows.

"Baby!" he blurted, snapping me out of my thoughts.

"What, Lah? Damn! You made me drop my pen and pad." I bent over the seat to pick everything I dropped.

"What you got a pen a pad for? Kori, bring your ass home now!"

"Okay, sheesh Lah. I was just trying to help!"

"I don't need you helping with this shit. We ain't been married but two weeks and already, you trying to make me a fucking widow!"

I threw the pen and pad in the passenger seat. He was really starting to piss me off. "Oh, shut up. You're not going to be a widow. Are guys even called that?"

"Yes, guys can be widows—fuck all that! Come home, now!" he barked in my ear.

I was trying to start the car, but nothing was happening.

"What the hell? My car won't start—"

CRASH!

"Agghhhh!"

"Kori?! Baby! Are you there?!"

To Be Continued...

Made in United States
Orlando, FL
02 May 2023

32709984R00121